Ryker wiped th
wondered who
made him for a c
for some pimp k
girls. Could ha
When you go u
you are automatically on a lot of shit lists.

The police came. A patrolman with two rookie cops. Ryker made a concise statement and left. He didn't want to be around when the brass arrived. He had a lot to do before the long, restraining arm of officialdom caught up with him. For the first time in weeks he felt motivated. And when he felt motivated, he felt mean . . .

By the same author

The Sniper
The Hammer of God

JACK CANNON

The Smack Man

GraftonBooks
A Division of HarperCollinsPublishers

GraftonBooks
A Division of HarperCollins*Publishers*
77–85 Fulham Palace Road,
Hammersmith, London W6 8JB

A Grafton UK Paperback Original 1991
9 8 7 6 5 4 3 2 1

Copyright © Nelson De Mille 1975

ISBN 0-586-20459-8

Printed and bound in Great Britain by
Collins, Glasgow

All rights reserved. No part of this publication may
be reproduced, stored in a retrieval system, or
transmitted, in any form, or by any means, electronic,
mechanical, photocopying, recording or otherwise,
without the prior permission of the publishers.

This book is sold subject to the condition that it
shall not, by way of trade or otherwise, be lent,
re-sold, hired out or otherwise circulated
without the publisher's prior consent in any
form of binding or cover other than that in
which it is published and without a similar
condition including this condition being imposed
on the subsequent purchaser.

*NOTE TO THE READER

The Smack Man was first published in March, 1975, by Manor Books and was written by Nelson De Mille. Jack Cannon is a pseudonym for Nelson De Mille.

The Smack Man is part of a series of six previously published books now published by Grafton Books under their original titles. They were originally published in the USA as follows:

The Sniper	Nordon Publications/ Leisure Books	August, 1974
The Hammer of God	Nordon Publications/ Leisure Books	October, 1974
The Smack Man	Manor Books	March, 1975
The Cannibal	Manor Books	April, 1975
The Night of the Phoenix	Manor Books	June, 1975
The Death Squad	Manor Books	August, 1975

Each of these books has been revised and updated by the author. In the Nordon Publications/Leisure Books editions, the main character was Detective Joe Ryker. In the Manor Books editions, the main character was Detective Joe Keller. For continuity, all of the new Grafton editions use the name of Joe Ryker for the main character.

We hope that the original fans of Detective Joe Ryker and Detective Joe Keller, as well as new readers, will enjoy these updated and revised books.

THE SMACK MAN

ONE

Benny Schwartz was a wreck. He stood, or to be more exact, slouched against the brick wall of a building on Avenue B in lower Manhattan. He stared vacantly at the passing pedestrians and street traffic. Occasionally a radio car would cruise past and slow down as the cops spotted Benny. On one occasion, the cop in the passenger seat—the cop closest to Benny—held his nose as he gave Benny a look which is usually reserved for puddles of vomit or dog shit on a new rug.

The cops on the Lower East Side saw lowlifes every minute of every day; they had to deal with black lowlifes and Spanish lowlifes, old derelicts and young white hookers. They dealt with deformed and handicapped people, who, through no fault of their own, had sunk to the bottom of society. They arrested people in the muck, human beings on the skids, the great unwashed, the mob, the homeless, the insane, the rabble. They spent their working hours with the dregs and the scum of the earth: the citizens of the

THE SMACK MAN

Lower East Side. Of course they also saw the rich, the talented, the beautiful, the artistic, and the well-educated, but not often professionally. There was not too much in between. Only the residue of Ukranian, Jewish, Italian, and Czech families who lingered on, trapped in their crumbling rent-controlled apartments, afraid to leave, terrified to live. There was no silent majority here. It wasn't that kind of a neighborhood. You either had it or you had it done to you.

And then there was Benny Schwartz. The cops hated Benny and his kind even more than they hated everybody else. They hated Benny almost as much as they hated the rich, Wall Street gentry infiltrating the neighborhood. Benny was neither black nor Hispanic, he was neither old nor was he a cripple. He was not deformed in the usual sense of the word. The average cop figured you needed some good reason for being a scumbag: a healthy white guy had no excuse.

Benny Schwartz had no excuse. He was a lowlife because he was a junkie. Nobody made him a junkie; he just decided it was a lifestyle he was comfortable with.

Benny Schwartz stank. His bare toes poked out of one shoe and his dirt-black heel out of the back of the other. His blue jeans were black with city grime and soot; his undershirt was gray with food, dirt, and grease. His hair was matted, that is, never combed so that it grew tangled and twined around itself. His black beard was matted too. It held remnants of food, lint, and bird shit for weeks on end. The long black beard and hair and the Semitic features, coupled with the burning rheumy eyes, reminded religious cops of a fiery biblical prophet. But to most he was just a junkie scumbag with no excuse.

THE SMACK MAN

Benny had badly yellowed teeth, frighteningly unhealthy sallow skin and a slight infection in his left eye that never seemed to heal.

He also had a set of tracks up and down each arm and each leg. He shot junk into his hands, his fingers, and his penis. One vein in the left arm was collapsed.

All of these afflictions were hung on a very thin five-foot-eleven-inch frame. Benny Schwartz looked like he had only a few days to live, or more accurately, like he had died a few days before but didn't know it.

Benny yawned lazily as he moved further back into the shortening shadows of the noonday summer sun. He was hungry, he supposed, because he hadn't eaten in two days. He reminded himself to steal some candy bars later.

He picked at a loose scab on the back of his left hand. The scab moved slightly as he got his dirty fingernail under it. He smiled as the large flake began to yield and part from his flesh under the insistence of his nail. Yellowish plasma seeped out of the open sore after the scab was ripped off.

Picking at the scab wasted a few seconds, important seconds, because Benny was waiting. Waiting for his connection. Today was a big day. For the last year he had been strictly a buyer. A user. A junkie. Now he had good bread in his pocket and he was going to score big. A kilo. Roughly two point two pounds. He was going to become a seller. A pusher.

Everyone on the street knew this and everyone wondered where Benny got the money and where he was going to push the junk. The market was already parceled out. It took more than a big score to become a pusher; you had to have customers. And if you took somebody else's customers you were asking for trouble. Big trouble. Especially from the niggers—the Haitians, the Jamaicans, the locals. But Benny had customers, and he wasn't going to step on any other pushers' toes, either. He wasn't going to threaten other pushers' territories. Benny would push the stuff where no other pusher could ever hope to sell it anyway. Benny Schwartz was going to push junk to the hookers—the same hookers who got their smack in rationed quantities from their pimps. The hookers who, through their pimps' payroll deduction plan, paid inflated prices for low-quality junk. These girls were going to be Benny's new customers.

Benny would step on the key, breaking it up into nickel bags. The price he would charge would vary, depending on the market and the quality. The stamp-sized nickel bags were sometimes sold half-full as treys—three-dollar bags. In any case, when the original kilo was cut with milk sugar, quinine, or both, and parceled into nickels and treys, the profits were enormous. So Benny was going to solicit the solicitors. He would not take a quick trick or a back-alley blow job for a bag. Benny wasn't interested in sex. Only money —money to buy more junk. The girls weren't interested in him either, he thought, hawking up a mouthful of phlegm. Their johns were many things, but filthy wasn't usually one of them. The girls had enough leeway on the job to pick men who didn't physically repulse them. They turned away some dwarfs, men with extreme deformities, limp-wristed, consumptive young men, syphilitics, and others whose peculiar problem might be disagreeable. Some girls, however, took on all comers regardless of race, sex, age, handicap, or country of origin. They were equal-opportunity hookers. They usually had AIDS.

THE SMACK MAN

Their do's and don'ts weren't many. Their job was considered semi-skilled and did not take a great deal of training. It came naturally. Their commandments, handed down by their pimps, were fewer and easier to remember than the biblical ten. They were simply this: Thou shalt have no other boss but the Man. Thou shalt work every day in any weather the Man says. Thou shalt never get pregnant. Thou shalt not steal from or hold out on the Man. Thou shalt never bear witness against the Man in court. Thou shalt never give it away for free. Not even to Robert Redford.

It was that simple. Any dumb whore could remember it. Girls who crossed their pimps usually didn't live to tell about it. The best they could hope for was a bad beating.

The big pushers sold directly to the pimps. Sometimes the pimps pushed a little junk themselves on the side. Nobody sold to the hookers. It was more trouble than it was worth. Hookers came to the Man with their day's receipts, then they got the junk. That was one of the ways the pimps controlled their stables.

Pimps also maintained their control by bailing the girls out when they got picked up by the cops. The dumb bitches also got a beating afterward for being so stupid.

Hookers were also protected from predatory young pimps trying to start their own stables or trying to cut into the competition's territory.

Anybody looking at the system would say, hell, it's not worth it, baby. Go into business for yourself. Some of them did. But the vast majority of New York's hookers were owned and operated by black and Spanish pimps.

Of course, there were problems. When the girls held

out on the money, it was a capital offense and it meant rough stuff. More rough stuff meant more pad money for the cops to turn their backs. And since fewer cops were on the pad these days, the ones who stayed on wanted more money for the risk. The price of Lincolns, Cadillacs, Mercedes, and gasoline was way up. So was the price of flash clothes and skag. Profits down, unhappy employees, crazy South American crack dealers, disappearing clientele fearful of disease, and rising expenses. The classical precursors of bankruptcy. The pimps were worried. They were being alphabetized out of business by a combination of DEA, FBI, and AIDS.

Now Benny Schwartz was about to deliver another body blow to the sick industry. He was about to break with tradition and sell a pimp-owned hooker a nickel bag. A little man like Benny Schwartz was about to rock what was at one time a very big boat. In the 1970s when business was good, Benny Schwartz would have gotten off with a good beating. Now with the business in bad shape and the pimps grim, anyone who fucked with the system was liable to get the death penalty. The man who was about to dump the kilo on Benny was retiring to Jamaica anyway. He would be gone by nightfall. Benny knew he could always find pushers who for one reason or another would sell to him, even if they knew what he was going to do with it. Some pushers were bigger and badder than the pimps. They didn't care. Some were obscure, small-time operators too insignificant to attract anyone's attention. Others, junkies themselves, never realized in their drug-bent minds the penalties involved in supplying a man like Benny. The South Americans, of course, lived by their own rules. To them, blacks, and black pimps in particular, were of no account.

Benny Schwartz scratched his crotch. His contact was late. He looked across Avenue B to Tompkins Square Park.

The two-block-square park in a sea of crumbling tenements was actually more of a mirage than an oasis. It looked like a green haven in the hot summer sun, but to the close observer, the green was poisonous: spotty clumps of grass grew haphazardly; the trees bent low, tired and dusty; the shrubs, purple and bristling with thorns, squatted like dwarves taking a shit. Still, compared to the way it had been in the early 1980s, Tompkins Square Park was a paradise.

Benny pushed himself off the brick building, not knowing that it had once been used by the Immigration and Naturalization Service as a processing center for the immigrants who had swept through the Lower East Side in the 1890s. When the Bohunks, Bohemians, and, for all anyone knew, Belgians came to their senses and stayed home in droves, the building fell into disuse. It was revived in the 1960s by the Black Panthers as their headquarters. Now it was a condo, financed by Citicorp, boasting studio apartments that sold for a minimum of a half-million dollars. Such was progress on the Lower East Side, and 143 Avenue B, which Benny Schwartz used as a backrest, was a paradigm of all that was right—and wrong—with the area.

Benny Schwartz didn't know any of this or care. He was originally from Long Island and thought of Manhattan as a foreign country. Besides, he had more important things to think about, especially Trevor

Wellsley, his contact. A tall Jamaican from the slums of Kingston, Trevor might be mistaken for an ordinary, ganga-toking Rastaman, but that would be a fatal mistake. Trevor, like his 3,000 counterparts, belonged to one of the twenty "posses" which had sprung up like cancer in the tropical slums of Jamaica and metastasized to the festering jungles of New York. The posses had started small, farming, importing, and distributing marijuana—ganga. But by virtue of hard work and a crazed capacity to kill, the Jamaicans had clawed their way up the crime ladder. They were now into crack, horse, and flake; they had out-gunned the local motorcycle gangs to become the number-one gunrunners in town. They were tough, shrewd, and fearless—they shot before they saw the whites of your eyes or the pigment of your skin. They gave Benny Schwartz the creeps, but he didn't have any choice. If he wanted to score the heroin, he had to hook up with the posse.

Trevor Wellsley, his dreadlocks bouncing to the tune of some inner music, came walking cool and slow through the park. He was wearing skintight jeans, a Western-cut jacket, plaid shirt, and a wide-brimmed cowboy hat adorned with a lizard-skin band and an array of brightly colored feathers. His boots, made of the hide of some grotesque and endangered species, added three inches to his six-foot-four-inch height. To Benny he looked like a walking version of the Empire State Building.

Benny shuffled up to him, an Igor cringing before the master; they made eye contact briefly. Benny flinched. "You got the bread on you, man?" Trevor asked in a low, rumbling voice.

THE SMACK MAN

Benny nodded. "Sure." His voice was listless. Dead.

Somebody going to clap this dude, Trevor thought. He'd be dead meat by winter. "Where you gonna carry the shit, man? A key ain't no nickel bag, you know."

Benny shrugged. He knew what he must look like. His two hip pockets had been cut out by a straight-edge razor while he had slept on the subway. He had made the mistake of putting a rag in one pocket and a pack of gum in the other. Two petty thieves had mistaken the bulges for money. In any event, a kilo wouldn't have fit there anyway. He had two tight side pockets. His ripped tank top couldn't conceal anything; it barely covered his torso. He was embarrassed. "I never thought—"

"You dumb motherfuck. Why you so stupid?" Trevor said. "I'm carryin' around a K of shit here and you can't even cop it."

Benny shrugged again.

Trevor looked around. Across Avenue B was a bodega. "You get your ass in that there spic grocery store and get a quart of soda in a bag."

Benny nodded and moved off. A few minutes later he came back with a quart bottle of Dr Pepper in a large brown grocery bag.

Trevor was getting nervous and impatient. "Drink some of that shit, man."

Benny nodded and unscrewed the aluminum cap. He wrapped his thin hands around the brown bag and drank.

To make things look cool, Trevor was going to take a few slugs too, but seeing the condition of Benny's

THE SMACK MAN

teeth and lips, he decided against it. "Let's walk, man."

They walked south on Avenue B, then east on Second Street, which was lined with tenements in various stages of collapse. Suddenly, the pusher turned off the sidewalk and crossed the street. Benny followed. A black wrought-iron gate stood between two of the five-story buildings. Trevor opened the gate and motioned Benny into the narrow alley. Benny followed and closed the gates behind him. They walked over ancient cobblestones until they reached the small common backyard area. Trevor looked around. Nothing was stirring, except a few rats. He knelt in a clump of chest-high ragweed.

A good exchange was an invisible exchange. Even if a narc was around, Trevor knew that he was clean as soon as the junkie had scored.

Benny knelt beside the black pusher. This was a critical moment. This was when a junkie could get ripped off if he looked easy. But Trevor was retiring and didn't want trouble. He was cool. He had at least eight inches and eighty pounds on the sick-looking young man, and a long-barrel .45 in his pocket that could knock down a telephone pole at 100 yards. Trevor was in control and that was the way he liked it.

Benny thought he should say something. "Matthew said you had good shit, man. Matthew and me been tight a lot of years, man. He said you was okay. Good shit."

Trevor understood that this was supposed to tie them together through mutual acquaintances. He ignored the remarks. "Let's see the bread, man," Trevor said.

THE SMACK MAN

Benny shook his head almost violently. He knew the drill. "Gotta see the shit, man."

They'd been there too long already, Trevor thought, impatiently. He reached behind his back under the loose-fitting western jacket and ripped a plastic bag loose from the tape that held it to the small of his back. He unfastened a twisted wire from around the opening of the bag.

Benny quickly wet his dirty finger in his mouth and jammed it deep into the bag. He put his finger to his nose and sniffed the brownish powder. He licked it all off his filthy finger. He waited a second or so. "Okay, man. It's good shit." He said it listlessly as if it didn't matter. But it did. It mattered very much.

"Then lay the bread on me, man," Trevor said, anxious now. He was always angry with himself when he laid good stuff on a loser like Benny. He wanted to bash the little prick's head in, taking the money *and* the junk. But there'd be no time to sell it. The plane would leave soon. He held out his hand. "Now, man. Now."

Benny fumbled in his tight side pockets. He brought out a fistful of sweat-soaked bills and held them out.

Trevor took them with a grimace. They actually stank. "Where you get this stuff, man? A snatch bank?" He stood. "I don't want no trouble with the likes of you," he said. "I could clap you with my fucking puppy in the right here and now." His puppy was the long-barrel .45, also called a yeng, a gong, or a tool. To clap was to shoot, and in this case the sound of one hand clapping was very loud indeed; Benny felt his balls draw up inside him; he began to shake. But the Jamaican dropped the key of heroin at his feet,

THE SMACK MAN

and with the infinite arrogance of a tribal chief, stalked off, his back an easy target.

Benny licked his filth-encrusted lips and crawled crablike toward the plastic bag of dreams.

He retrieved the kilo and dropped it in the brown paper bag next to the bottle of Dr Pepper. Then he got slowly to his feet and moved off through the weeds. He pressed his left forearm against his T-shirt. A recent knife wound had opened again and was starting to bleed.

TWO

Detective Sergeant Joseph Ryker awoke to the ear-shattering ring of the telephone. He sat bolt upright and tried to breathe, but there seemed to be no air in his bedroom. It was like gasping for breath in a furnace.

Coughing, he staggered from the bed and picked up the phone.

"Yeah?" he choked.

"Oh, Joe. Did I wake you?"

He looked at his watch: 7 A.M.

"No, Ellie," he said to his ex-wife. "Just give me a minute."

He pitched the receiver down on the sweaty sheets and, hands out like a sleepwalker, he felt for the air conditioner. It was making a low buzzing sound, but no air was coming in or going out. Ryker turned it off, then tried to open the window. The muscles across his hairy chest rippled with the effort, the cords on his bull neck stood out, and he turned beet red. But it was only when he heard the beginning of a tear in his groin and felt things popping down there, that he remembered he had nailed the window shut.

"Fucking Peg," he grumbled to himself. Peg was a biker's chick who lived downstairs. She had sold him the air conditioner.

He ran a hand through his shaggy black hair. It was damp and greasy; he shoved it out of his eyes and sat naked on the bed.

"Yeah, Ellie?" he said into the phone.

"I'm sorry. Am I interrupting anything?" she asked.

"Not a thing," he said. "Though I'm real hot."

"Oh, well, I'll let you get back to your, uh, guest," Eleanor said. Since their divorce almost seven years ago, Eleanor had taken an unnatural interest in his sex life. She also began calling Ryker at all hours of the day and night. They were "communicating," she told him in answer to his snide questions. And he had to admit it was true. He talked to his wife more now than he ever had during their marriage. Of course, "communicating" was much safer when they were separated by years and 650 miles.

"How's the ad biz?" Ryker asked. "Condoms and compacts selling well?"

"Very well, indeed," Eleanor said brightly. She refused to get mad and play his game.

"Well, as I told you, Ellie, I'm real hot, so if there's nothing more—"

"Wait, Joe," she said. "Just a minute. Tell your uh, girlfriend that it's important. I want you to come to Chicago."

"Sure, babe," he said. "Soon."

It was a game they played, promising to visit each other, then conveniently forgetting.

"No, I'm serious. I have a proposition for you," she said.

"Sexual, financial, or illegal?" he asked.

"I'll tell you when you get here. You have tickets waiting for you at Kennedy. United Airlines. Saturday. Eight A.M."

"What's this all about, Ellie?" He was intrigued now.

"Let's just say that I want you to share in a great moment of my life."

"Yeah?"

"I'll call you soon," she said. "Love you."

"Yeah," Ryker said, hanging up. When she had pleaded with him to give up his job and go with her to Chicago he had been stunned. He was a policeman, for God's sake, a New York City detective, he had told her. He couldn't just walk out on the job to become some kind of househusband, while Eleanor blossomed as an advertising executive. She had cried, but she had left—left him unable to comprehend why she wasn't content to be Mrs. Joseph Ryker.

Ryker went to the small, rusty air conditioner and talked to it softly. "Work, motherfucker, or I'll throw you out the window."

He pushed the on button. A small hum, then silence, then a slow draft of cool air.

"That's better," Ryker said.

An hour later, Ryker sat on a hot, empty bench in Tompkins Square Park, watching the action, while the August sun baked the concretelike ground around him. A lot of junk changed hands in this park, but Ryker wasn't interested in junk. He was interested in murder. Homicide. Shortly, a man who knew about a homicide that the police hadn't even discovered yet would sit down next to Ryker and talk.

Ryker waited. He removed his Porsche sunglasses and rubbed his eyes. His tan cotton suit was dark with sweat under the arms. He put his glasses back on and lit a foul-smelling cigar. The smoke from the cigar hung in the motionless air.

Ryker stretched out his legs. He was familiar with the park, comfortable with it. Many years before, he knew, Tompkins Square Park had been typical of the citywide system first introduced in the mid-nineteenth century. Parks were designed as sylvan retreats for native-born Americans recently come to the big city from the family farm to earn a factory wage. But the tidal wave of immigrants from such outlandish places as Russia, Romania, and Transylvania quickly overwhelmed the earlier park-goers and the newcomers seized the parks for their own use. Parks became family-oriented places of recreation and ersatz retirement homes for the elderly, who sat in the sun, playing chess and telling lies about the old country. These immigrants, what modern bureaucrats would call the working poor, had things pretty much their own way until the late 1960s. Then a new phenomenon arrived on the Lower East Side—the hippie.

Hippies swarmed to the area, attracted by the incredibly cheap rents, other hippies, and a complete breakdown of traditional moral and social values. It had energy, man, they said. It was groovy. It was cool to be a part of the solution, man, not a part of the problem.

The hippies lasted about two years and were eventually murdered, raped, and OD'd into American mainstream life by savage packs of Hispanic drug dealers. Armed with automatic weapons and huge, vicious Rottweilers, the Spanish–American war for the park was finally won by the dealers. Manila Bay was revenged, and Tompkins Square Park became Farmer Juan's Open-Air Drug Market. Ole.

In those days—the early 1970s—even ball-breakers like Ryker found excuses to stay away from the park. Then in the mid 1980s Operation Pressure Point throttled the small-time, big-crime junk trade. Pressure Point turned the whole area into a police substation, with eight cops on every corner eyeballing the scene. Four months of police harassment and very few howls from the civil liberties people later, resulted in a miracle. The cops had actually managed to scrape away a layer of excrement. There was still shit in the outhouse, but it was old, less pungent shit. Women with babies, kids with skateboards, and codgers with chessboards began to reappear, bringing an end to the nightmare and the beginning of a new normalcy. Or seminormalcy, for the area now attracted punk rockers, new-wavers, and the most despised urban phenomenon, the yuppie.

The park had been saved, but the people who should have used it were being forced out of the neighborhood by the new ruling class, the gentry. Gone were the $80-a-month apartments, the Ukranian restaurants that gave free meals to the poor, Jimi Hendrix's studio, and Mrs. Goblinsky, her cats, and grandchildren. In a year or two at most, the park would sport uniformed nannies promenading about with tow-haired tykes, while working mothers were out tolling in a new ERA and letting Friedan ring.

Ryker blew a smoke ring in the still air and followed

its progress with about as much enthusiasm as he had watched the park rise and fall over the years. The smoke ring rapidly dissipated, and Ryker was suddenly looking at a tall black man approaching. He wore a white linen suit with red stitching on the lapels and pockets. He sported a pair of pointy white patent-leather shoes with taps. His shirt was a diaphanous purple affair open at the collar; gold chains cascaded down his bony, hairy chest. The outfit was completed by a large, floppy, wide-brimmed felt hat. He could have been a guest star on "Miami Vice."

The black man did a graceful little pivot, folded up like an erector-set drawbridge, and settled down on the bench. Neither man spoke for a few seconds.

The black man slid closer to Ryker and whispered, "You Ryker—right?"

"Yeah," Ryker said. "Where's the body, Rodney?"

"Hold on, man. Let's move a little slower. I got to get some reassurances here first."

"The only deal I can promise you is that if you're covering up a homicide I'm going to throw your ass in the slammer, and I'll see to it that it stays there 'til it's old and wrinkled," Ryker said, looking straight ahead.

Rodney shook his head violently. "No way, man. No and no. I'm tryin' to be a good citizen here. You see? I'm tryin' to do my civic duty, understand? I don't want a hassle with you, man. I get enough of that."

"Pimps do," Ryker said. "It's a part of the job."

"I'm a talent scout."

"Right. Okay, talent scout, what's the deal? You got a court date coming up? Is that it?"

"No, man. I'm cool."

THE SMACK MAN

"Money?" Ryker wondered if business was that bad.

Rodney wanted to say that he made more in a day than a police sergeant makes in a month, but he knew that would be a very stupid thing to say. "No, man. I'm doin' okay."

Ryker was becoming impatient. "You looking to finger somebody, Rodney? You giving somebody up?"

"Shit no, man." *Shit* came out as two syllables. "Shit. I never done that in my life. I never give a dude up."

Ryker took off his glasses and looked at the pimp for the first time. Rodney looked back and saw a pair of crazy green eyes set on each side of a thin, aquiline nose. The jaw was hard and suggested impatience. "Then what the fuck do you want? You want a mayor's medal? I'm not here to pull teeth, motherfucker. I'm here to listen to you tell me a story," Ryker said.

Rodney, conscious of Ryker's hard eyes, began slowly. "Thing is, man, if I tell you what I want—I gotta tell you a lot of shit I don't want you to hear unless I get reassurances."

Ryker sighed. "Let's get something straight. You know about a murder. You didn't do it or you wouldn't be here talking to me. Okay. You don't want anything in return except immunity. Immunity because maybe you're a little involved in something on the edges of this murder. Right?"

Rodney scratched his head. His conk was wilting in the sun. "Yeah. I guess that's it. But I ain't involved in no murder. Not on purpose, I ain't."

"Let's have the story, Rodney. I'm a busy man," Ryker said.

THE SMACK MAN

Rodney played with his jacket cuffs for a minute, then spoke softly. "I got a dead hoor in my pad."

Ryker's face remained impassive. So that was it. He wanted somebody to tell him, we believe you if you say you're clean. He also wanted someone to remove the stiff, no doubt. The weather was real warm. "So?" Ryker prompted.

"Well, yeah, I mean it's like this." Rodney looked up at the sky. "I mean I coulda just took her out tonight and dumped her, you know? But then I'm thinkin'—look, Rodney, you a pim—a talent scout. Always been. Never had nothin' to do with murder. See? Never wasted a dude in my whole life. Understand? So I don't need this shit, man. You know? Maybe I go to the police and they can straighten it all out, you know?"

"So?"

"So, I come home last night—"

"Last night?" Ryker said. "You waited long enough to call."

"I had to think about it, man. I mean I don't go runnin' to the cops every day with my problems, you know? I mean here I am telling you this shit and you're makin' up charges in your head already. I mean you're sayin', let's see—how long can I put this nigger in jail? You know? I mean you gotta get off my case, man, or I'm gonna dry up."

"Spill it," Ryker said. The sun was as hot as a stolen BMW.

Rodney scratched at his knee. He thought for a minute. "Okay. So I come home and one of my—clients—a model, you understand—she's layin' on the couch there and she's been shootin' junk. You know? I mean I never use the shit, man, but she musta brought it in and she's layin' on the couch, man, with like the needle still in her thigh, you know, and she's dead. I mean she is *dead.*" He looked sideways at Ryker.

"So? She OD'd," Ryker said. "Thousands of junkies OD every year. A lot of them die. What do I care? What makes you think this was murder? Why are you bothering me with this shit?"

"Look, man, this was no OD. I seen OD's too. They look like they're hearing Gabriel's sweet horn in their ear, some of them. She don't look nothing like that. Besides, most of the shit is still in the syringe, man."

"Maybe she was doing a second or a third when she went down," Ryker said.

"No, you don't see. The look on her face, man. Somebody give that girl some bad shit. Now that's murder, ain't it?"

There'd been cases like this before, Ryker thought. If something in the junk killed somebody, it might have been put there on purpose. "Could have been an air bubble," Ryker said.

"Yeah, maybe. But I don't think so. This girl knew how to use a needle, you know?"

"Okay, homicide, then. Go on," Ryker said.

"Yeah, murder. That's what I thought. So I figured I might as well call you. I got your name from a buddy. This dude said you was straight, man. So I got a problem. I got this bitch in my house with junk and shit, and I can see the cops coming down on me. And they say, you got no visible means of support, you know? How you afford this here fine place, my man? And you got junk here. And this girl looks like a pross and she got tracks on her thighs and you been busted

THE SMACK MAN

before for pimping and some other small shit and now we got your black ass for murder and all that bad shit. You see?"

"Life sucks," Ryker said. "You gave her that shit? I mean these 'models' of yours don't cop on their own, do they? You don't run a loose stable, do you, Rodney?"

Rodney looked embarrassed. "Hell, no, man. I run a damn tight stable. Any bitch gets outa line with me, I slap her upside the head—" He stopped. He realized that he was incriminating himself. "No. I don't score for my ladies. I don't want junkies—"

"Cut the bullshit," Ryker said. "These girls don't work for you because of your good looks. They work for you because they're junkies. You tell me where you cop for them, and I'll take it from there. Okay? No charges. No fingers pointing back at you."

Rodney shook his head. "No, man. I thought about it. The dude I cop from is straight. He's my main man. We tight. Look, the others had the same shit, and they all right. Listen, I been suspectin' for a few weeks now that some of these bitches of mine been copping on their own. You know—they is high when they should be comin' down. So I ain't gonna give up my man. He got nothing to do with it."

"You mean you don't want to be the dude that supplied the junk that killed this whore. So you're jiving me with this shit about them copping shit on their own. Some tight stable. Who's gonna push to a hooker? Only the Mafia and the Dominicans would have the balls for that, and they don't deal nickel bags to whores, anyway. So where does that leave us? Other South Americans? Jamaicans?"

Rodney shook his head. "I don't know, man. I don't

know. You see—right away I'm gettin' set up for the long ride, man. I didn't have nothing to do with the shit she shot up, man. Understand?"

Ryker nodded. "Okay. You touch anything in your apartment?"

"Hell, no. I see her all laid out and I don't touch nothing. I seen police movies, too. I slept someplace else last night. I wasn't gonna sleep in the same place with no stiff."

Ryker got up. He pulled his pants loose from his crotch. "Come on, Rodney. I got one call to make, then we're going to your house."

THREE

Rodney's living room was filled with expensive but tasteless furnishings. Simulated ermine and tiger skin covered everything. Plush white long-shagged throw rugs and tiger-skin cushions lay scattered across the floor. Two ebony African masks hung on an otherwise bare wall. On the white fur couch, sunk into the deep luxurious cushions, was a very pale black-haired white girl. She was naked and lay in an obscene position with her pelvis thrust into the air. Her back was arched like a bow and the top of her head was sunk into a pillow. Her buttocks barely touched the couch and most of her weight was distributed between the soles of her feet and her head. She looked like an ornamental Japanese bridge.

Ryker moved over to the couch, bent over the coffee table, and examined the exotic, erotic scene of her death. The girl, about eighteen, had an agonized expression on her face. Her arms were thrown out as though she had just begun to struggle, then decided it wasn't worth it. There was a length of medical tubing wound around her left thigh; an eyedropper and a box of wooden kitchen matches lay on the coffee table. A half-filled hypodermic needle lay next to her on the couch.

The girl's clothes were thrown casually about on the floor. Apparently she had stripped and stretched out on the voluptuous fur to shoot up. A pack of cigarettes and three empty bottles of grape soda stood stolidly on the coffee table. Ryker could see ugly red scars on her thigh below the tubing. He ran his finger along the outside of the nearest thigh. At least one vein had collapsed from frequent injections. Probably more. He figured the other thigh, up against the back of the couch, was just as bad. He looked up and down the length of the arched body. The hooker's black pubic hair stood out in sharp outline against the smooth skin; her nipples and aureoles, once no doubt red and tantalizing, were now slate color: dead. Her lips were purple—a result of the same cold, blue color underneath her bright red lipstick. Her body was full and well-fleshed for a junkie, Ryker thought. Youth can overcome anything for a while, he decided. Her mouth was pulled back in the rictus of death. The white skin and purple lips and eyelids were framed by the pitch-black hair, giving her face a sort of sexy, vampire look. Ryker straightened up and turned to Rodney. "She live here?"

"Hell, no. I never let none of them live here. She's one of the ones had a key, though," Rodney said.

"How many you running, Rod? How many have keys?"

Rodney looked proud. "I got eight. Now just my

main girl, Julia, got a key. She sort of the straw boss of the girls."

"What did she think about this honky bitch having a key to the Man's pad?" Ryker asked.

Rodney looked defensive. "She's cool, man. No sweat. She don't care."

"We'll see about that."

"Man, if Julia wanted this bitch gone, she'd be gone. No sweat. She don't have to kill her."

Ryker shrugged. He knew Rodney was probably right. Jealousy was rarely a motive for murder in this business. He began thinking about the business. Eight girls, each of them bringing five hundred bucks a day, seven days a week. They got to keep the cost of their junk, their rooms, their clothes. Four grand a day, week in, week out. Not bad. No taxes and all you had to do was cruise your posts a few times a day. Maybe if you were nice, you let a freezing girl into the car for a quick drink and a little heat in the winter. Or in the summer you let the sweating, wilting hooker in for a quick beer at the car's bar. That's if you were soft. Rodney didn't look soft. He looked like a tough boss.

"She was a moneymaker, huh?" Ryker asked.

Rodney looked almost sad. "She had her shit together, man. Never got the clap, never got pregnant. Hardly ever got rounded up by the pussy posse. She could talk real high-class talk, man. Used to get the big-money dudes. Couple hundred bucks sometimes, a grand once. Bitch never hustled a sailor in her life, understand? She had it all together."

"Then what the fuck did she need you for?" Ryker asked.

Rodney looked offended. "I'm the Man, man. She needs me. They all need me. A bitch ain't nuthin' without her Man. They too dumb to handle it themselves."

Ryker moved to the door. He could hear footsteps in the hall. Before the bell rang, he opened the door. His boss, Lieutenant Fischetti, and two detectives, Fernandez and Williston, were with him. A half dozen uniforms stood behind them.

"Wanna get laid, Lieutenant?" Ryker said without letting them pass. "Corpse's a little cold, but so what? It's a hot day."

"Your jokes are never very amusing," Fischetti said from the doorway.

"But you're a married man, so you already know what dead pussy is like."

Fischetti didn't answer. The less he said to Ryker, the better they both liked it.

Williston, a black detective, poked his head in the door and looked around. "This looks like a pimp pad."

Rodney looked at the black cop with a mixture of hate and fear. He forced a smile. "This is my model agency, brother." He held out his hand as though he wanted to slap palms in the familiar black greeting, even though both men were at opposite ends of the room.

Williston scowled. "Don't give me that jive-brother shit." He turned his back on Rodney.

Rodney felt this was all a show for the white cops. He would try to talk to the black detective alone later.

Fischetti set up an efficient crime-scene routine by stationing a uniformed sergeant at the door with a crime-scene log, plastic gloves and booties for everyone. He chewed Ryker out for entering the apartment before procedures had been established, then lapsed

THE SMACK MAN

into silence. He had already received the rundown from Ryker by phone, and he could do nothing until the technical people arrived.

The first to show up was Latent Fingerprints, then Forensic, then Crime Lab. They began working quietly. Finally, two police photographers arrived and set up their tripods. They began snapping in color; their pictures always made them the hit at a party. The pictures were strictly for police eyes only, but everyone agreed that they were too good to keep hidden. The photographers' wives said that they couldn't understand the fascination these ghastly photographs held for people, but they were happy with the social life such ghoulish pictures seemed to generate.

All the newcomers stared at the contorted naked body for a few seconds, then went about their business.

A few newsmen drifted into the building and stood in the hall. The big, uniformed sergeant at the door barred their entrance. Fischetti gave them a short statement designed to make them lose interest and go away. He told them the deceased was a junkie whore who had apparently OD'd. The reporters decided that the case was a piece of shit. There were a lot of junkies who OD'd. Nobody seemed to need another one. Most stories of OD's never even made the papers. It was a sad, depressing, totally ordinary problem in the city. This was going to be a nowhere story unless there was a twist or an angle: JUNKIE PROSTITUTE OD'S IN PIMP PAD. They played with it; it kept sounding boring. NAKED JUNKIE HOOKER OD'S IN PLEASURE PAD. Better, but not quite. NAKED PROSTITUTE DIES MYSTERIOUSLY. Naw. The newspaper men might have to work on it.

THE SMACK MAN

The TV and radio reporters knew that their air time was too valuable to even mention it. They thanked Fischetti and left.

Ryker sat back in a fake-ermine-covered lounger that had just been tossed by the crime lab. "Williston."

"Yeah, Sarge."

"Sit down with Rodney here and take his statement. Not too much jive talk, please—it confuses the white stenographers," Ryker said.

Williston smiled. "Right off. I mean, right on."

"Fernandez."

"Sarge?"

"Get on the horn and see what's keeping the fucking medical examiner this time. Fucking doctors think the world's got to wait on them." Ryker didn't like doctors. Their egos were as big as his own.

"Right," Fernandez said.

Another pair of detectives from the precinct detective unit arrived. Parsons and Dooley. Ryker stretched his big frame out on the lounger and watched the familiar scene unfolding in its predictable manner. Latent was dusting everything that might give a clue. Disqualifying prints were taken from the dead girl, Rodney, and Ryker. The crime lab was gathering the normal quota of lint, hair, and cigarette butts. Forensic sat around and waited for the medical examiner. Their jobs were closely interrelated.

Ryker could see that several of the patrolmen, as well as Parsons and Dooley, were becoming increasingly bitter as they poked through Rodney's luxurious apartment. If Williston wasn't there, Ryker knew, there would be a lot of antiblack talk. But he also knew the problem wasn't black or white. He had been in Mafioso townhouses that made Rodney's place look like a tenement. He'd been in the condos of wealthy WASP embezzlers and stock manipulators that looked like a movie set. He'd seen the homes of wealthy Greeks who smuggled everything from gold to aliens. He'd been in the hotel suites of French and South American narcotics importers. In fact, just about every ethnic group in New York had their specialty. No, the problem wasn't black or white, but criminal versus honest citizen. Did crime pay? It sure did.

Ryker thought of his own seedy apartment, and wondered if maybe he wasn't in the wrong end of the business. He had a sudden impulse to crush the pimp's skull with a patrolman's nightstick. The feeling passed. He lit a cigar and threw the burning match over his shoulder; he flipped ashes on the white rug.

Rodney was becoming increasingly nervous as he watched everyone poking around his pad. Williston had to offer to blow his fucking head off a few times to get Rodney's attention. Detective Billy Parsons, with a wife, four kids and a mortgaged two-family house in Queens, couldn't take much more. He called out from the bedroom to Dooley. "Hey, Chuck. You ever see a motherfucking gold-tipped walking stick? This fuck's got a fucking gold-tipped walking stick. You ever see a mink belt? Come check this shit out."

The younger patrolmen in the room would get one of two things out of this experience, Ryker thought. Either they would go after the parasitic bastards like Rodney with more vengeance or they would decide that crime did pay. As he watched the faces of some of the cops, he felt that he knew what decision each of them was making in his own mind.

Rodney watched, too. He knew what was happening. He wondered if they would try to pin something on him. The apartment was clean of all dope as far as he knew. Also he had stashed his piece, a big mother of a .357 Magnum, at a friend's house. Two of the cops had found his large collection of pornography, however. They were intrigued by his homemade video cassettes and fascinated by the large color glossies of the sex parties he had thrown. A few of the girls were obviously under age; at least one of the posed S&M scenes wasn't posed at all. It was a young runaway whom Rodney and his pals had really bound and whipped. He wondered if the cops could tell; sweat began forming on his face. He knew he'd have a very rough time operating in this neighborhood in the future.

The assistant medical examiner finally arrived. He nodded briefly to Ryker, whom he recognized, and walked directly to the body. He pronounced her dead, which made it official, but not any more dead than she was already. He began filling out his reports.

"Cause of death, Doc?" Ryker asked, without getting up. The background noise in the room subsided. Fischetti walked out of the bedroom and stood attentively by the door.

This was the assistant M.E.'s big moment. "I don't know," he said.

"Come on, nobody's going to point and laugh if the autopsy shows you were wrong. We need something to work with now. Take a guess, Doc."

THE SMACK MAN

The young intern, Dr. Needleman, shrugged. "Wasn't an OD. Victim was in apparent pain, as you can observe. Severe muscle spasms. I'd guess something in the hypodermic killed her. Something other than heroin."

"Like what? A poison? An air bubble?"

"More likely a poison. See the arched position of the body?" The doctor walked back toward the couch. "The arched back? Opisthotonus. Rigid extension of the muscles. Facial spasms, as well as an increase of muscle activity before death. Then we have the characteristic appearance of anoxia due to apnea. In other words, suffocation. Spasms of the thoracic muscles."

"So what are you saying?" Ryker asked. "Somebody slipped an Alka-Seltzer in her douche and she giggled herself to death?"

The doctor smiled wanly. "No, my guess is someone slipped strychnine in her heroin. A fatal dose of strychnine. At least a hundred milligrams."

Ryker rose from the lounger. The room was very quiet. He approached the young doctor. "This is a homicide? Not suicide?"

"Strychnine is neurotoxic. People don't commit suicide with any neurotoxic unless they get a kick out of muscle spasms and pain. Look at that body." He pointed to the bowed figure. The backbone was in an impossible position; the mouth told a chilling story without uttering a word.

"With strychnine, sometimes the muscle spasms are so severe that the bones break," Dr. Needleman said. "They're snapped by the muscles. Very painful. Anyway, an experienced addict can take small regular overdoses of heroin and commit suicide quite pleasantly without the convulsions that characterize a single massive overdose of heroin. That's the way an addict would terminate himself."

Ryker was still staring at the contorted naked body. The hypodermic was about half full and a purple spot on the thigh showed that she had been administering an injection immediately preceding her death. But maybe the two weren't related. He looked at the soda bottles. "How about that soda? Could someone slip strychnine in there?"

The doctor shook his head. "No. The stuff can't be taken orally by accident. It's not like arsenic. It's very, very bitter. A hundred milligrams is about the size of an aspirin, let's say. To dissolve that much even in a bottle of this sweet junk would still be noticeable." He pointed to the hypodermic. "The lab will find the stuff in there. It mixes very well with heroin; it's colorless, odorless, and crystalline. It won't change its chemical composition when mixed or heated either. So when a junkie heats his shit, the strychnine is not affected. Also, its bitterness is hidden in the heroin's bitterness, so that if it's sniffed or tasted, the heroin still seems good."

"You sound like a junkie, Doc," Ryker said.

"You work in this city long enough, you start mainlining the stuff right into your brain," Needleman said.

"Good," Ryker said. "I can't wait for the lab, so why don't you taste a drop for us now? There's plenty left in the hypo."

The doctor laughed. "I'm not afraid of the strychnine. A little taste won't kill. In fact it's even used

THE SMACK MAN

medically as a stimulant to the nervous system in small doses."

"So chow down on some. I'm in a hurry," Ryker said.

Needleman shook his head. "No, I'm not that expert. The bitterness of heroin and strychnine are too similar. We'll have to wait for the lab report. And there's always the possibility of serum hepatitis or AIDS from the needle. I don't need it."

"I'll wait for the lab," Ryker said, with mock disappointment. "But what ever happened to the doctors who used to expose themselves to things like yellow fever in the interests of medical science?"

"They're dead," Needleman said.

"Since this stuff mixes so well with the heroin," Fischetti cut in, "and you say in small doses it's a stimulant, then isn't it possible that it could be used to cut the heroin without any willful intent of poisoning somebody?"

The young M.E. scratched his head. "Yes," he said. "I've heard of it used that way, but it's not a very economical way to cut the stuff. I mean milk sugar is so much cheaper and goes a hell of a lot further. Quinine is sometimes cheaper too and goes further. Strychnine is illegal, hard to get, expensive, and can only be used in such small quantities that you can hardly cut a bag enough to make it worthwhile. I'm not a detective, God knows, but if I were, I'd say murder. Willful and premeditated—with forethought and malice, and all that good shit."

Rodney had been listening very intently with one ear as Williston took the last of his statement. He didn't look happy.

The other cops suddenly regarded Rodney with new hostility.

Fischetti scratched his head.

Ryker dropped his cigar stub on the white rug, ground it out, and said, "Somebody's slipping some bad shit in the good shit."

FOUR

Ryker and Fischetti stood at the low concrete wall overlooking the East River. Below them, people were playing tennis in the early afternoon sun.

Ryker propped his elbows on the wall, leaned back, and chewed on a dead cigar. "I think this may turn out to be big."

"I don't think so," Fischetti said. "Dead junkie whore. Period. I'm putting Fernandez and Williston on it. They're more than capable of handling it."

Ryker shook his head. "I want this one."

Fischetti knew this was coming. "Why? So you can bust the balls of a bunch of black pimps? I know you've been looking for an excuse to go after them for a long time, Ryker."

Ryker bit into his cigar. "Look, Lieutenant, I don't like the fuckers. Black, white, or green. You understand?"

Fischetti fought down his anger. "Just forget it." He looked out across the river. A rusted freighter leaving the Brooklyn docks was headed for the open sea. The bright sun shining through the haze gave everything the look of a very artistic movie, shot with filters. Sometimes, especially when he had to deal with Ryker, Fischetti wanted to be on a freighter like that, without a care in the world.

"Look," Ryker said. "There's more to this than a dead whore. Somebody is pumping strychnine into the pipeline. This could become a fucking epidemic. It could be big, and I want a piece of it."

Fischetti scratched his head. "I'll tell you what—if another junkie dies, I'll buy it. But personally I think it's a one-shot deal. Somebody wanted her dead. Maybe Rodney's main woman."

"Maybe. Meanwhile, Rodney has taken a liking to me, so let me finish the interrogation today. Then I'll wait and see," Ryker said.

Fischetti pursed his thin lips. Ryker always seemed to get his way. "What do you have in mind?"

"I'm just going to make him round up his stable. I want to question all of them. Then I'll be cool. Fernandez and Williston can take it from there."

"Okay. But no muscle."

"Lieutenant, have you ever known me to use muscle?"

"Have you ever heard the words *excessive force* and *police brutality?*" Fischetti asked.

"Never heard them before," Ryker said. "Anyway, don't worry about me. Tell Captain Perez to worry about his patrolmen. When the locker-room bullshit gets out on Rodney, every rookie cop in the precinct will want a piece of his ass or a piece of the action."

Fischetti knew Ryker was right. Vice was pretty

much immune to the affluence and high living of the pimps. They either took their cut if they were crooked or they busted the pimps and their girls. The average patrolman, though, never got into the world of prostitution. The closest they got was occasionally running a prostitute off their beat. Or writing out a ticket for a pimpmobile parked one and a half inches too close to a hydrant. Sometimes they even gave the car a little push to get it in summons range. Petty harassments. Tickets. Nick a pimpmobile fender once in a while.

"I'll pass that on to Captain Perez," Fischetti said, squinting at the freighter, willing himself aboard.

Rodney was waiting for Ryker in front of his building; two uniformed policemen stood on either side of him. The pimp didn't look too happy; neither did the two cops. They were wondering if they would get a chance to beat the shit out of Rodney. Their straight middle-class sensibilities had been offended by what they had seen upstairs, and they were almost pawing at the pavement in anticipation of getting the pimp alone.

"Bring him here," Ryker said.

The two patrolmen shoved and prodded Rodney across the street to where Ryker was standing, giving him a final, unnecessary push.

Ryker drew on his cigar. "Okay, you big, bad, motherfucking pimp, your ass is still hanging out, so you got a lot of cooperating to do before you can walk. There's two cops up in your place that have snowflaked you bad, Rodney. They laid an ounce of primo shit on you. They also planted a hot gun in your dresser and they would like to hide the Liberty Bell in your bathroom if they could. They want your ass, and

THE SMACK MAN

they'll get it unless I tell them you're being cool with us. You listening to me?"

Rodney nodded. He knew he should have dumped the damned bitch in the river.

"Okay. Where's the pimpmobile?" Ryker asked.

Rodney motioned back toward the apartment.

"Where's your stable at?" Ryker asked.

Rodney looked at his gold Rolex. "Six is at Saxon and two around a little dive called the Sweezy Hotel."

"Good. Let's go." Ryker pushed the pimp toward the apartment building.

Down the block from the apartment, blocking a service entrance, was a huge, customized, lavender Eldorado with a heavy chrome Rolls-Royce grill. It had white pinstriping, white enameled moon hubs and a special continental kit on the trunk with the word "Rod" spelled out in glittering letters. Ryker walked up to it and rubbed his eyes. He took out his sunglasses and put them on. "What the fuck is this supposed to be—a grape?" He peered inside. The seats were covered with a deep plush synthetic zebra skin.

The pimp unlocked the door for Ryker, then went around and got in.

Ryker opened the door, and got in the back. "Pull up in front of your building," he said, then sat back and relit his stale cigar. He dropped the match on the plush carpeting.

Rodney was pissed at having to play chauffeur to a pig. He started the car, slammed on the accelerator, and stamped on the brake a few seconds later. He looked at Ryker in the rearview mirror, but the cop was smoking serenely, dropping the ashes on the zebra-skin seat.

Ryker ground out the cigar on the thick rug. "Okay, Rodney, the Saxon Hotel. Make it quick."

Two streetwalkers were talking to each other in front of the seedy SRO hotel near Bowery. Rodney had become less sulky, and he turned around to face Ryker. "You see that shit? 'Stead of hustling, they bullshitting all goddamn day. What these bitches got to talk about all day, huh? Big mouths always yapping. Lazy no-account—"

"Okay, I get the point. Are they yours? Get them in here," Ryker said.

Rodney lowered the tinted window. "Hey! Get your butts over here."

Both girls looked up with a start. They ran toward the gleaming lavender Cadillac. Ryker motioned them into the back seat with him. One of them opened the door cautiously. The only white man they could think of who would be chauffeured around by their Man was some kind of connected Eye-talian guy. They figured they were about to change owners. Ryker moved over and they slid in. They stared at him. He damn sure didn't dress like a wise guy and he didn't look particularly Italian.

Ryker lit a cigar. "Okay, Rodney, let's go."

The girls looked at him curiously as the car pulled away from the curb.

"I'm from the Salvation Army, girls. I'm here at Rodney's request to talk to you about the wages of sin—which as you know ain't shit," Ryker said.

Both girls gave a little shudder, but they said nothing as the car rolled on.

They were anemic-looking and heavily made up, white chicks. They sported identical swept-back hairdos; their skirts were short-short and showed a bit of ass. Their jewelry was plastic and too large. Very low-class, Ryker decided. Nothing like Vivien, the dead girl, had been.

"Why you two always bullshitting?" Rodney said. "You gonna get a good slap upside the head—"

"Shut up!" Ryker roared. "We're here on my fucking business. Not yours."

Rodney got sulky again and began driving too fast. He screeched to a halt on the next block and picked up a blowzy redhead. The heavy girl slid in beside him. "Where's Wanda?" he snapped.

"She's got a date upstairs," the streetwalker whined through her chewing gum.

Ryker looked at the decayed Sweezy Hotel, then opened the built-in bar and took out four cans of cold beer. He passed them around to the girls and drank one himself. No one spoke. Rodney sat gripping the steering wheel.

Finally Ryker crushed his half finished can and dropped it on the carpeting. "How long does this bitch take for a trick, Rod? That's why you're not doing so well. That's how you lose money. Time is money. You need a good business manager, somebody to kick ass," Ryker said, belching.

Rodney had been listening to Ryker with rising but impotent anger. But at the mention of a manager, he perked up. He let go of the steering wheel and turned around. "You want a job, man? I can guarantee you five large a day and a piece of the action. What you say to that?"

"I say, shove it up your ass. I have a thing going that makes your operation look like a suburban wife-swapping club," Ryker lied.

THE SMACK MAN

Rodney was all ears. "Yeah? What you got, man? You want a partner?"

Ryker winked. It was generally a good idea to let a criminal think you might be a little crooked, too. You heard a lot more interesting things that way. "Later."

Rodney winked back.

Ryker looked at his watch. "Okay. Vice raid, Rodney. I can't wait for this bitch while she's giving a record-breaking blow job." He opened his door and got out into the heat.

The three whores were trained to keep their mouths shut, and they just sat in confused silence as their boss followed the strange man.

"You ever been on a vice raid before, Rodney?"

"Not this end of one, man."

They entered the small, seedy hotel. A spidery old man slouched across the clerk's desk. He regarded the odd couple curiously. "Help you?"

"Prostitute and a john. Little while ago. What room, pop?"

"We don't—"

"Cut the shit," Ryker snapped.

"Well, there were a few," the old fart said, scratching the fringe of white hair around his bald head.

Rodney described his hooker, and the old man remembered her.

Ryker took the key and they rode up the old elevator to the sixth floor.

"Don't lean against the elevator wall," Rodney said. "The cock-a-roaches will eat you alive."

Ryker straightened up.

They stepped out into the hall and looked at the room numbers as he walked. The hotel was dimly lit, run-down, and foul-smelling.

THE SMACK MAN

"Fucking roaches would starve to death up here," Ryker said.

"Naw," Rodney said. "They eat the rats."

When they found the room they wanted, Ryker said, "You like movies?"

"Sometimes," Rodney said, warily.

"I hate 'em," Ryker said. "The last one I saw was about ten years ago. Some kinda asshole tough guy went around ramming his shoulders into doors and knocking them down."

"I seen movies like that," Rodney said, still wary.

"Well, I always wanted to know if it really worked," Ryker said. "Knock that down with your shoulder. Back up and run at the motherfucker."

"Hey, man, we got the key," Rodney said.

"Fuck the key," Ryker said. "Do it."

One look at Ryker's cold green eyes convinced the pimp that he'd rather have a bruised shoulder than a busted head, so he did as he was told. He retreated about ten steps and ran head-on at the door. He hit it with considerable force and bounced, like a pinball off a cushion; he fell to the floor.

"See?" Ryker said, looking down at Rodney. "It doesn't work. Just phony Hollywood shit."

Rodney got up shakily, rubbing his shoulder. From inside the room they could hear the hooker and her john suddenly get real quiet.

"But one thing that does work," Ryker said, "is my size twelves." He raised his foot and smashed the door right below the lock.

The door splintered like matchwood, the bolt ripped from the casement, and the ruined door swung open, slamming against the wall.

Ryker stood a few feet inside the small dingy room.

THE SMACK MAN

A naked couple lay on the bed staring. "Excuse me," Ryker said. "I happened to be in your neighborhood and I'm demonstrating vacuum cleaners. Are you the lady of the house?"

The girl screamed.

"Police!" Ryker roared. "Shut your fucking mouth. Get up! Get up!"

The middle-aged man was half scared and half relieved; he sprang out of bed. "Let's see your identification," the john stammered.

"Shut your yap. Pay the bitch and beat it." Ryker made a threatening move toward the man. He figured him for an out-of-towner.

The john began dressing hurriedly; the hooker pulled the sheets up around her bare breasts.

Rodney walked in behind Ryker. At his back were a dozen other people who had rushed from their rooms to rubberneck. The whore saw Rodney and looked relieved but puzzled. She couldn't decide if it was a raid or not. She decided it wasn't. Vice raids had become as rare as hoedowns in New York City. You had to be running an S&M, B&D club catering to chickenhawks to qualify for a real raid anymore.

Ryker chased the spectators off, then he screamed at the john again. The girl began crying; Rodney screamed at her; Ryker screamed at Rodney to shut him up. The room was a madhouse of confusion. Ryker was having a damn good time.

The john fumbled with his billfold, while Rodney watched him shrewdly. The man ripped off a hundred from a wad and threw it on the bed. Rodney scratched his chin, taking stock of the situation. His eyes fell on a half-empty bottle of scotch on the dresser. He looked at the girl under the sheets.

THE SMACK MAN

"So what you doin', girl?" he said. "Drinkin' on the motherfuckin' job?" He counted off on his fingers as his voice droned. "Tellin' me you never got more than fifty and this dude is laying a large on you. Number three, why you take so long to satisfy this gentleman, here? You get paid by the trick, not by the fucking hour."

Ryker told the pimp to shut up again. "My business, not yours," he reminded Rodney. He turned to the girl. "Come on, bitch. No time to be shy. Get your ass up and dressed."

The hooker scrambled out of bed and began dressing quickly. Ryker watched her for a moment. She had tracks on both thighs. She was pretty enough, much like the other three in the car, except she was younger, no more than sixteen, he guessed. A child, really, Ryker thought.

He walked over to the bureau and took a long pull from the bottle of Chivas, then turned to the john, who didn't know if he was going to be busted or not. "Beat it," Ryker said. "Don't forget to get an AIDS test before you get home to the wife." The man grabbed his jacket and bolted out of the room, past the seedy bums who were watching the hooker get dressed. Ryker chased the audience off again. "What a fucking place," he mumbled to himself.

Ryker looked down at the hundred-dollar bill on the bed. If he gave it to the girl, Rodney would have it. He picked up the money and looked at Rodney who was looking at the money. "Yours?"

Rodney looked indecisive; he licked his lips. "Yours."

"For the PBA Fund?"

"Yeah."

THE SMACK MAN

Ryker stuffed the bill in his pocket. "You get your ass to the precinct by noon and make sure you fill out a pledge form for it and get a receipt. Understand?"

Rodney was confused. He thought Ryker was going to cop it for himself. "Yeah. Okay, man."

The young hooker was standing by the bed, dressed and waiting for instructions. Ryker threw the bottle of Chivas at her; she caught it. He walked toward the door. "Come on," he said. "We're gonna have us a whore convention."

FIVE

"I keep my prime bitches uptown," Rodney said primly. "This trash is just my downtown branch office."

The four hookers looked angry, but they didn't say anything. Ryker smoked while the big lavender Cadillac with the Rolls-Royce grill picked its way across town to Eighth Avenue, then headed north.

On the way up Eighth Avenue a police car began to harass them. A favorite sport of a lot of patrol-car cops was called "nick the pimpmobile." Another dent or two on the blue-and-white didn't make much difference, but a nice crease in the candy-apple, metal-flaked, hand-rubbed finish of a customized Lincoln or Cadillac could ruin a pimp's whole day. Ryker flashed his tin as the cops drew alongside the pimpmobile and yelled to them. They stared at him in wonder but dropped back.

Several pedestrians did double takes as the lavender pimpmobile with the black dude, the four hookers, and the white guy cruised past. Ryker was thoroughly enjoying the ride. "You drive this boat right, Rodney, or I'll get you another ticket."

The big Cadillac turned onto West Fifty-seventh Street and stopped in front of the Henry Hudson Hotel. Rodney double-parked at Ryker's insistence, and everyone got out.

The odd entourage walked down the long, narrow lobby to the elevator bank. The hotel had long since ceased being a real hotel. Its inhabitants were mostly transients, hookers, and welfare families. Some rooms had efficiency kitchens; the hallways smelled of urine and strange foods. Some of the floors contained office suites and were rented out to legitimate businesses, and some not-so-legitimate businesses. Three floors had been leased by the overcrowded Roosevelt Hospital a few blocks away. The space was used mostly as an abortion mill. There was also a drug rehabilitation clinic in the building and a methadone treatment center in the basement. A few apartments were used as a nurses' residence. It was a very strange potpourri of people who passed each other in the lobby every morning.

The elevator came, and they entered along with a welfare mother, a doctor, three nurses, and an Indian woman in a sari holding two infants. On the eleventh floor, Ryker and company stepped out into a threadbare carpeted hallway. The overpowering smell of curry almost made Ryker choke; the odor of stale fish oil assailed them from another doorway as they began walking. Ryker followed Rodney down the narrow, slightly uphill hall. Rodney kicked at a door.

"Who's there?" It was a shrill young voice.

"Who the fuck you expectin', Rose Ann?"

THE SMACK MAN

The door opened. A girl about eighteen years old stood there in a frilly sequined teddy. Rodney pushed past her, and Ryker followed. The four hookers filed in behind the men. They shrugged and shook their heads in answer to Rose Ann's silent question.

Inside the small white room were two beds. A girl slept in one of them. "Where's the rest of them?" Ryker asked.

Rodney motioned to an adjoining door. "It's a double room, see? They's two more in there. These four," he motioned to the four girls he and Ryker had picked up, "they got two double rooms across the hall. Two suites. Four rooms. Eight beds. See?"

"That's pretty quick adding, Rodney. You really keep the girls in style, I see," Ryker said.

The four girls who had not been told anything about Vivien's death figured they were being sold along with Rodney's entire operation. Rose Ann, a heavy, very dark kid, figured the same thing. The sixth girl slept on. She snored occasionally—the sleep of pills or heroin, Ryker figured.

The big cop poked around the room. It was as filthy as it was childlike. Open boxes of candy lay everywhere. Children's dolls were sitting up on the chairs and dressers. Clothes lay scattered among a heap of stuffed animals. All the accessories which the girls had brought to the room were pink and feminine-looking as if to reaffirm their girlishness. He looked into the small bathroom. A pair of pink lace panties lay under the sink; a reddish brown menstrual stain blotted the crotch; a cockroach was crawling on the blood. Ryker closed the door and turned around. "Get the other two in here."

The pimp snapped his fingers, and one of the girls

THE SMACK MAN

bolted through the adjoining door. She came back a few seconds later with a sleepy-eyed redhead in baby-doll pajamas.

"Thelma, where's Nancy?" Rodney demanded. He was always suspicious that the girls turned tricks on the side or that they brought johns back to their makeshift dormitories when they were supposed to be sleeping.

"I can't get her up," Thelma said.

"Lazy bitch," Rodney growled. "I'll just beat on her ass for a while. That'll get her up." He moved toward the door.

Ryker pushed him aside and walked quickly into the adjoining bedroom. On the bed, under a single sheet, was what must have been Rodney's number-two girl. With her eyes closed and makeup off she looked almost wholesome. There was, however, the beginning of a pained look on her face. She had long, naturally golden hair. Ryker stared. There was no rising and falling of the sheets. He moved closer to the bed and grabbed the top of the sheet, and pulled it down with one sweep of his hand.

Nancy lay on her side with her back arched like a bow. Except for a pair of black panties pulled down around her ankles, she was naked. Stuck into her raised hip, looking very much out of place on the soft flesh, was a plastic hypodermic needle.

Ryker had called for reinforcements. The scene at Rodney's luxury pad was repeated again in the seedy hotel. The difference, besides the location, was that now a swarm of reporters jostled and jockeyed each other for position. Only a fool had trouble seeing the connection now. This had the makings of a good story.

Rodney moaned to anyone who would listen that his business was ruined. He also cursed and screamed at the already hysterical girls for buying their own junk. Ryker threatened to throw him out the window if he didn't shut his fucking mouth.

Ryker had also informed Rodney that his apartment, the two suites, and Vivien's separate room down the hall would be padlocked until further notice. He told the pimp to make other sleeping arrangements for himself and his flock. Rodney was regretting more and more his decision to play good citizen and go to the police. He felt sorry for himself. He took some comfort in the fact that even if he hadn't told them about Vivien, he would still have had to worry about getting Nancy's body out of the hotel and into the river. It would have been nearly impossible.

Rodney started thinking about who his enemies were, a natural thing for a man to do when his luck suddenly turns bad. Was somebody poisoning his girls for revenge? Who? The Mafia? Nobody from that enterprising group had even made him an offer that he couldn't refuse. Another black pimp? He couldn't remember stepping on anyone's patent leathers recently. Pissed-off cops, setting him up? He didn't know.

He did know that his two best girls were no longer fucking their brains out for him, and that was an economic disaster. The other girls were panicky and showed signs of desertion. If somebody had it in for him and he couldn't even protect them, who needed him? On top of all this, the cops had his number and would harass him until they got tired of it or until he paid out a lot of money. His car was slightly soiled and very ticketed because of this prick Ryker, and he was sure it had been towed away by now because he was double-parked for hours. That meant a trip down to the dock where the impounded cars were kept by the police. It also meant fines and towing charges of almost three hundred dollars. To add to his misery, he was sure that he would find that the tow-truck guys had abused his car on purpose. The paint job and body work had cost him five thousand dollars the last time this happened. He sat on the edge of the bed and almost wept as the police went over the suite. They tossed the room across the hall, too. There was no need to snowflake these rooms, either. There was plenty of junk around.

Now on top of all this, Ryker was going to lock him and his girls out. Legally, Ryker could do this without worrying about the courts. A crime scene was a crime scene, and no judge would deny Ryker's right to keep the locks on for at least a week. Another harassment, since it really wasn't necessary to lock them out.

Ryker questioned the girls. No, they didn't know who Vivien and Nancy copped from. They had had pushers try to sell to them from time to time, but they always said no. Rodney provided. Rodney was the Man. A few of the girls even hinted that Vivien and Nancy maybe got what they deserved if they were copping on their own. The played-out hookers obviously didn't like the two pretty dead girls.

Rodney's main girl, Julia, was picked up and brought to the station house. She seemed straight enough. No real motive for wanting Vivien and Nancy dead and Rodney ruined. Julia called the dead hookers white trash, and said she wasn't at all jealous of either of them. She explained, "How the motherfuck do a pimp's girl get jealous, man? He balls all the white chicks who work for him. I don't give a shit, man." It sounded reasonable to Ryker.

At eleven-thirty, a detective announced that he was taking all the girls in for possession. Small quantities of heroin and marijuana had been found in all the rooms. Rodney put his head in his hands. How did a simple, hard-working talent scout get himself into all this trouble? He saw his business going down the tube.

Ryker came over and put a consoling hand on Rodney's shoulder. "You did the right thing, Rod. A good citizen should always go to the police when he knows of or has witnessed a crime. We need more people like you to come forward. I'm going to see about a mayor's medal for you."

Rodney wanted to say, "You fucking white honky pig motherfucker. You gonna put my ass on welfare yet." Instead he said, "I'm finished, man. Wiped out."

Ryker looked concerned. "Chill out, Rod. You seem to have a way with women. You could always become a hairdresser."

Rodney jumped up and ran into the hall. The reporters were being held at bay at the end of the hall near the elevators so that the police and lab people could walk freely between the suites. Rodney was going to run over to them and blurt out his sad story of police brutality, figuring the local papers would make him look like a folk hero. They always did. Perhaps he could get help from the scores of wild-eyed reverends who were constantly looking to show up the cops and scream about racism, all the while making themselves rich, snotty media stars. Naw, he thought, fuck 'em.

He took the fire stairs down eleven stories and walked over to the clerk's desk. He got himself a room far away from Ryker's rampaging detectives. He was temporarily out of cash, but at least he had a pocketful of stolen credit cards. He took his key and walked outside. His car *was* gone.

He bought a liter of peach-flavored schnapps at a small liquor store near the hotel and retired to his room. The bitches at least had lodgings for the night, compliments of the City of New York. Maybe he would bail them out tomorrow, maybe not. If the judge released them without bail in the morning, they could find their own shelter someplace. He wasn't interested. Fuck them. Fuck Ryker. Fuck everybody. He uncapped the bottle of schnapps and drank. It had been a bad day.

A wall of stale, furnacelike air hit Ryker in the face, sucking the breath from him. He felt beads of sweat erupt all over his body, while noxious fumes from long-dead creatures assaulted his senses. Dust, billowing clouds of it, settled on his white nylon shirt, making him look like a grainy newspaper photo of himself. It was 12 A.M. and Ryker was home.

He kicked an empty bottle of Jack Daniel's out of his way, ignoring the camouflaged-colored living room with its broken-down, filthy furniture, and headed directly for the bedroom. Cancerous lumps of dirty clothes sprouted everywhere; gray, tangled sheets were strewn about at random.

Ryker threw his tan poplin suit coat on the floor

beside an identical one he had doffed the night before, tore open his sweat-encrusted white shirt and stood silently for a second, as if in prayer.

"Work, you cocksucker," he said to the air conditioner. Then he punched the button for "Frosti-Kool," and the machine emitted a low, strangled moan.

"I mean it," Ryker growled.

The moan was louder now.

"No shit," Ryker warned.

Suddenly a blast of air blew across his bare chest like the cool caress of a woman. Ryker closed his eyes and imagined what it would be like to be comfortable again. The noonday temperature had been 85, but the humidity was close to 100 percent.

Ryker unbuckled his belt and let his pants fall to the floor. His tattered gray boxer shorts went next. If I live to retire, he told himself, I'm going to spend my summers in Antarctica, sitting on an icebag, wearing nothing but an undershirt.

He remained standing in front of the balky old air conditioner until most of the sweat had dried from his body. Then he went into the bathroom and turned on the cold water in the shower.

The day had wired him out, made him shaky, hinky, and tense. All that pussy had affected him, too, he thought, and it was his own damn fault. It had been two weeks since he had gotten laid. He stepped under the cold shower and lathered his groin, thinking about his part-time girlfriend, a full-time call girl named Beverly Kim. He had met her around the time of the Chinatown cannibal case and had been enjoying her company ever since. Tall, exotic, erotic Beverly, he thought, off on a month-long tour of Europe with some rich old fart. Her price was twenty-five large, plus expenses, clothes, and jewelry. He couldn't order her not to go. Hell, he thought, she'd be a fool not to go. And to ask her not to leave him would be an admission that he cared for her. He did, but he didn't want her to know it. She was a pro, he was a pro, and pros did things professionally, he thought. There was no room for sentiment, no place for passion. He stopped lathering his groin and rinsed off.

As he stepped out of the tub, he felt a sharp pain in his foot. "Son of a bitch," he said aloud, kicking an inch-long screw into the corner of the bathroom.

He toweled off, wondering where the fuck a huge screw like that had come from, and worse, what it was supposed to be holding together. If Ryker had been a philosophical man, he would have viewed the screw as a metaphysical symbol. Instead he related it to his meager sex life, thinking he had been screwed without being screwed.

In the bedroom, now cool by comparison, he opened his closet. On the left-hand side were five identical brown wool suits that he wore in winter; on the right, three identical tan suits he wore in summer. Two other tan suits were lying on the floor, ready for Freddy Choy, the Chinese laundry man, to work on. Between the suits were five long-sleeve white shirts and three short-sleeve white shirts. Hanging limply from a hook were five dark brown wool ties and three light brown polyester ties. The ties were already knotted and ready to slip around his neck. Ryker bought all his clothes from a fat Greek in Brooklyn who ran a small-time marijuana dealership and an odd-lot clothing store. He got a five-percent "professional discount."

THE SMACK MAN

Beverly Kim had called him a sartorial disaster, but since he wasn't quite sure what that meant, Ryker hadn't been offended. Clothes were clothes, cars were cars, cunts were cunts, he thought—it didn't matter what make or model you had, as long as you had it when you needed it.

He was straightening up the damp sheets when the phone rang in the living room. He debated letting it ring unanswered, then opened the door to the living room. The heat was intense. By the time he picked up the phone, all his work at cooling out had been ruined. He'd have to shower again.

"Joe?" It was his ex-wife Eleanor.

"Yeah."

"Am I interrupting anything?"

"No, Ellie. I'm alone."

"You'd say that anyway, wouldn't you?" Eleanor said. She sounded sulky to Ryker.

"What can I do for you, Ellie?" he asked.

"Are you coming out next Saturday?"

"Sure." He didn't sound sure.

"Really?"

"If you want," he said, unenthusiastically.

"I want. There's someone you have to meet."

"Who? The head media exchange creative art buyer?" Advertising titles were a mystery to Ryker.

"The what? No, I'm serious, Joe. I want you to meet Pancho," she said.

"Pancho?"

"Pancho—Eduardo Maria Gonzalez de la Toya y Marchando—Pancho," she said.

"Sounds like a disease," Ryker said.

"A very old family," she said.

"A very old disease."

THE SMACK MAN

"Joe." She was almost angry.

"Okay. Why in the name of tacos should I meet this guy?"

"You're going to be related. Sort of," Eleanor said.

"How so?" Ryker was mystified. "You going to adopt him?"

"No, Joe. I'm going to marry him," she said.

"No shit?" It came out before he had time to think. "What am I? Your father? I got to okay this wetback?"

"No racial slurs, please," Eleanor said, haughtily. "I just thought it would be nice if we could all get together as adults and . . . be friends."

"I got enough friends, Ellie," Ryker said. "Have a good marriage and send me pictures of the kids."

"Joe, that's hardly the attitude—"

"What the fuck do you want me to say, Ellie? Congratulations? You got it. Don't do it? You got that too."

"Maybe I just want to hear you say you love me," she said in a small voice.

"You got it," he said. "And *buenas noches.*"

SIX

At eight-eighteen the next morning Ryker mounted the well-worn granite steps of the East Sixth Street station house. Two hundred and fifty cops operated out of the roach- and rat-infested building that had been thrown up by the lowest bidder in 1898. In a spasm of public-spirited dementia, the original red-brick station house had been added onto in 1954—a white-brick west wing. Such a jarring clash of styles and building materials went unnoticed, and by the time Ryker had started working there, both the white bricks and the red bricks were black with soot and pollution. The unintentional harmony also went unnoticed. A police station is all function, no form.

Ryker nodded to the desk sergeant, Bronkowski, and headed up the stairs to the precinct detective unit squad room. Unlike his apartment, the squad room was cool and orderly.

Ryker walked into Lieutenant Fischetti's small glass and metal cubicle.

THE SMACK MAN

Fischetti looked up. "Oh, God."

"Only a sergeant," Ryker said. He leaned against the wobbly door post, enjoying his effect on Fischetti. Ryker could ruin the lieutenant's whole day just by saying hello. He sat down.

Fischetti tapped a pencil on the desk. "Yes?"

"I'm on this case," Ryker said. "And I need to know the word on the stiff hooker you found yesterday."

"Nothing yet," Fischetti said. "Could be a regular O.D., or it could be the same thing we're working on. The lab report will be in shortly. I talked to Lieutenant Carver up there, though. He said the girl's back was arched like a bow."

Ryker took out a cigar. "Sounds familiar?" He lit the cigar. "Well, I'm pretty sure Rodney is clean. You should have seen that silly motherfucker last night. His whole world just came crashing down around his perpetrator hat—"

Fischetti held up his hand. "Please, I don't want to hear about it. I have enough problems. You're going to get us a charge of police brutality and racial discrimination. Every fucking asshole with a mail-order divinity degree is going to be sitting on my head."

"Fuck it. I would have treated my father the same way if he was a pimp," Ryker said. "I have no use for those fucking parasites. White or black."

Fischetti nodded noncommittally. "Your problem, Ryker, is that you're not sensitive to the needs of minorities."

"Sure I am," Ryker said. "I'm sensitive to the needs of decent people who get fucked over by scumbags like Rodney. The good guys are a minority. The scumbags like Rodney are the majority in this town."

THE SMACK MAN

"Ryker, you're a dinosaur in a china shop," Fischetti said. "Don't you read the community-relations bulletins I put out?"

"Sure I do, Lou," Ryker said, using the abbreviation for *lieutenant*. "I read 'em every morning in the can. Then I wipe my ass with them."

Fischetti put his hand to his face to cover his eyes. He knew better than to even talk to Ryker, let alone lecture him. The sergeant was an anachronism, a living fossil. He was an honest, hard-working cop with a sense of purpose and a sense of justice that transcended politics. Ryker would bust the mayor or the president, if he thought they were guilty of something. He was out of touch with the sensitive, caring, helpful, colorblind image the department took great pains to project to the public. If he saw a handicapped, homosexual black woman with a Spanish surname promoted over a qualified white man, he said so. He didn't smile and beat his breast with pride at the vaunted humanity of the public bureaucracy. He hated anyone who put politics above safety or "sensitivity" above justice. Ryker was incorruptible, incorrigible, and a royal pain in the ass for a time-serving bootlicker like Fischetti.

"Why do you say these things, Ryker?" Fischetti asked. "Why can't you just go along?"

"Because I'm right and the rest of you are wrong," Ryker said. "Isn't that obvious by now?" Fischetti was silent. Ryker had saved his butt many times. He had the uncanny ability to cut through the bullshit and nail the perp.

"Let's get some people in here and brainstorm this thing," Fischetti said. "Fernandez! Williston!" he called.

THE SMACK MAN

"With a brainstorm like this," Ryker said, "our crops will curl up and die of drought."

Why me? Fischetti asked himself.

"As long as we're pretending to be organized," Ryker continued, "let's get Totten in here too."

"He's new," Fischetti said.

"Then maybe he's not contaminated by this place yet. Every time you make a decision, you step on your dick. No offense intended, Lieutenant," Ryker said.

Fischetti flushed with anger. He was about to say something, but Fernandez and Williston came into the cubicle. Fischetti grabbed the arm of his chair until his knuckles went white.

Ryker paid no attention to him. He was tired of Fischetti. Fischetti was an incompetent, an ass-kisser, and a pussy. Ryker spotted Totten and called him over.

Bob Totten was in his early thirties. Tall, blond, good-looking. He was an NYU graduate and had surprised and disappointed his well-to-do family by joining the force. Before he made sergeant, a few years back, he had earned a law degree. He believed in deductive reasoning. Clues. Statistics. He liked to think he could solve most murders from his desk. His heroes were fictional detectives who practiced the art of ratiocination. Logic.

Totten limped across the squad room. He had just gotten out of the hospital and was on very limited duty. His hospital stay was a result of a bomb blast at his last precinct uptown. Three bomb squad guys had been killed; Totten was lucky; he had been just far enough away to escape.

Totten was about as different from Ryker as a stiletto is from a baseball bat. They were both effective, but Ryker was an alley-prowler and a head-buster; Totten was a thinker and a planner. He reminded Ryker of his one-time partner, Bo Lindly. Lindly had been a college boy too, and it was his simple belief in the goodness of human nature that had killed him sure as shit. Somewhere in the back of his mind, Ryker thought he could do a better job with Totten than he had ever done with Lindly. He didn't want to think about it much, but he figured he owed it to Lindly.

Totten leaned against the door post; he looked pale and shaky.

"Come in, Totten," Ryker said. "The lieutenant wants you to try out for the police football team this fall."

"Fuck you," Totten suggested. "What do you want?"

"See?" Fernandez said. "See? Ever since he got those blow jobs from that ugly nurse at the hospital when he was in traction, he got mean. She kept biting his dick, man. Mean bitch."

"Isn't anyone going to offer me a fucking chair?" Totten asked.

Williston pulled a few chairs into the cubicle. Everyone sat.

Fischetti went over the case briefly. Despite the air conditioning the cramped cubicle got hotter. Fischetti picked up some papers. "All right. Here are the reports. Crime Lab found nothing in either place that shouldn't be there. It wasn't that kind of a murder. The small amounts of heroin that we found were cut with milk sugar. Street-grade, number 40 heroin.

"But here's the big one. The medical examiner's report says both deaths were caused by strychnine poisoning, apparently injected into a vein of the thigh in each case. Also, in each case it appeared to be self-injected; there were no marks or bruises to indicate a struggle. So the victims, then, believed that they were injecting heroin only. The solutions found in the needles showed a mixture of about half heroin and half strychnine. Strychnine was also found in the residue of heroin in the glassine envelopes at each murder scene. Only one smudged wild print was found, and although it might have been the pusher's, it's not enough of a print to even attempt to run it through the FBI. We asked them to try hand-matching thumb prints of heroin pushers. We might turn up something but it may take weeks. Any ideas?"

The men digested what they had so far. Ryker digested faster than most people. He spoke: "If any more junkies move on to the big shooting gallery in the sky we're going to have a real panic on our hands."

"Right," Williston agreed. "But is that good, or is that bad?"

"Who knows?" Ryker said. "Let's see, what could happen? A junkie makes his pusher share the skag with him? Junkies go out of town to score? The price of proven shit goes up? Who knows? It's hard to figure what could happen."

Fernandez spoke. "Maybe it could cause a run on the methadone clinics."

"Is that good or is that bad?" Ryker asked.

"Who knows?" Williston said.

Everyone sat and digested again. The case had been elusive from the beginning. A detective walking into a murder scene looks for two things: method and motive. In this case even the simplest thing, the method, had been elusive for a while. Motive was usually ascertained within hours. Sometimes minutes. A jealous lover, a robbery, a gangland slaying, a family argument—these accounted for over ninety percent of all murders committed in New York City. But nobody could even begin to come up with a hard motive here.

To make matters worse, there were no clues. Most murders were committed in person on the premises by the murderer. As long as the murderer was there, there was a better than even chance of turning up something—a hair, a print, an eyewitness, a cigarette ash. The Crime Lab flakes insisted that if the perpetrator even broke wind at the scene of the crime, they'd get a lead.

But remote-control killings like bombs, and poison, were few and far between—except on television, where that was the predominant type of murder. Now the police had a real-life remote murder. Poisoning by strychnine, administered unknowingly by the victims themselves, administered along with what was supposed to be a nice high. Two powders. Both white. Both bitter. Both crystalline alkaloids. One was called White Heaven in the trade. The other wasn't.

"Why is somebody shitting in the shit?" Ryker asked.

Williston answered. "Rodney thinks it was directed just at him."

"I don't think so," Ryker said. "If that was the case, the perp would have put the strychnine into Rodney's main supply. No, this was a random thing. A pusher is peddling nickel bags around town. Does he know it's bad shit? Did he buy it that way or did he lace it with poison himself? Who knows?"

"I'll agree with that," Totten said. "In fact I'll go a

step further. I'm saying that this is a plot. Somebody is trying to knock off junkies. That's the only thing that seems to make sense. Why put strychnine in a bag unless you want to knock off junkies?" Totten sat back in his chair. He seemed weak and dispirited. His words and thoughts were slow and abstracted.

Ryker considered. "Are we talking whore junkies or all junkies?"

"We'll know when the next stuff turns up," Totten said. "When we get something back on that hooker in Harlem, we'll know. If it's another strychnine poisoning, maybe this thing is directed against our sidewalk hostesses. Maybe some john got AIDS from one of them and now he's looking to get even. He doesn't care what happens to him anyway. He's a walking dead man. But if it's just a Jane Doe junkie that dies next time, then we have another thing here. We have somebody, maybe, who's going to do a civic deed and depopulate the great city of New York of its addicted citizens."

"Is that good or is that bad?" Ryker wondered out loud.

"It's bad," Fischetti snapped. "Homicide is bad. That's what our bosses are going to tell us, and that had better be our attitude."

"Well," Ryker said. "It's *one* solution to the problem, but in keeping with the department's enlightened approach to dealing with our unfortunate lower socio-economic victims of heroin addiction, as laid out by your own community-relations bulletins, Lou, it's not the solution those assholes would like to see, is it?"

Fischetti tapped his pencil. "That's the kind of talk that gets you into trouble."

"Who gives a rusty fuck?" Ryker said. "You know,

when I saw that first hoor in Rodney's apartment, lying there like that, I really got the hots for this case. Then the other one—Nancy. But now I'm wondering how I'll feel if a junkie with a rap sheet as long as my big dick turns up DOA I'm wondering if I give a shit, you know?"

Fischetti lit a cigarette quickly. His voice was edgy. "Well, if you feel that way," he said, "you might as well take yourself off the case. You only wanted to catch it so you could hassle the pimps, anyway." Fischetti looked very self-righteous.

Ryker leaned across Fischetti's desk. "Lieutenant, you really hurt me. I mean, I'm a good cop, right? Somebody says, 'There's a nut loose with a machine gun, Ryker, go get him.' I do it, right? But what are you telling me now? That I'm the only cop on the job who wants to see junkies die? Everybody else belongs to the Society for the Prevention of Cruelty to Junkies? You want I should catch AIDS from one of those pricks?" He turned to the three detectives in the room. "Does anybody here really have the heart for this case?"

Everyone looked at Fischetti. No one spoke, but the answer was clear.

"See, Lieutenant?" Ryker said softly. "See? Nobody gives a rat's ass if they catch the badass who's poisoning the skag supply. It would do wonders for AIDS pollution. In fact, I wish him all the luck in the world. Now on the other hand, if somebody was poisoning the supply of Jack Daniel's sour mash, I would be one pissed-off son of a bitch. So I guess it's all relative. Now you cán, number one, go out and find a couple of junkie detectives who would have a hard-on for this case, or two, accept the fact that we'll do the best we can without getting ourselves all worked up about it."

Ryker waited for an answer he knew he wouldn't get.

Fischetti was thin, balding, and shifty-eyed. He had a weak chin and a weak character. His lack of resolve was legendary. He had left his men's asses hanging out too many times because he put political considerations above the welfare of his men.

Fischetti lived in a make-believe world where everyone was liberal and enlightened. Now a cop had just told him he didn't give a rat's ass how many junkies died. And he, Fischetti, had the responsibility to discover how and why these murders were happening. He needed cops to do it. Hard to admit, but he needed cops. He didn't even like cops, and he was sorry that he had become one. He was unhappy that he had to associate with them. He wanted to be something else. He wanted to be at police headquarters above the grimy nitty-gritty precinct level. He wanted to be a crime advisor on the mayor's staff. He wanted to be away from cops like Ryker. But here he was, stuck with the Neanderthals. Even an educated man like Totten had become crass and foul-mouthed on the job. The big blue machine had teeth like a shark and could eat up even right-thinking humanitarians like himself.

"Give it your best," Fischetti said at last. "No pressure from me. No Unusuals to the P.C. I'll take care of that. No deadlines. No ultimatums. No ass-chewing from the brass. I'll catch all the flak. That's what you want, isn't it?"

Ryker didn't take anything Fischetti said at face value, but he decided to let the drivel go without comment. "Just one thing," Ryker said. "I need a fucking partner. What's holding things up?"

Ryker's last partner, Paul Sawyer, had retired with a 60 percent disability—at least 40 percent of which, he claimed, was directly attributable to Ryker. In truth, however, the twice-wounded Sawyer just didn't have the heart to go on after Ryker had uncovered a pervasive rottenness in the department, and had pulled the pin.

Fischetti allowed himself a thin smile. "No one wants to work with you." He almost gloated over the words. He had been saving this piece of news for the right moment.

"What the fuck are you talking about?" Ryker asked.

"Look, we put the word out last week," Fischetti said. "I even called Chief Lockman at Personnel yesterday. He's running it through the computer. In the meantime, we can get you a kid from the academy. They graduated a class from the criminal investigation course yesterday—"

"I don't want a fucking kid. I've had it with fucking kids," Ryker said. "When they're not getting themselves killed, they're trying to get me killed. I'd like someone who's been around long enough to know how to stay alive."

Fischetti stood up. "Maybe we can get someone from Narcotics. Those bastards have more manpower than they know what to do with, anyway. It might be good for this case, too."

Ryker considered. A narc had a lot of street savvy. That was a plus. More and more homicides were connected with drugs; or to be more exact, more and more big drug deals ended in homicide these days because somebody always tried to walk away with the money *and* the junk. There were a lot of amateurs in the business and that meant more gun play. On the minus side, there were a lot of narcs on the pad. It was the most lucrative of all pads. Between shakedowns, bribes, confiscated drugs, and confiscated money, a crooked cop in Narcotics could make more money than a crooked cop in any other division. So any man who would be willing to leave Narcotics for a PDU had either made his fortune already or was straight to begin with. In either case, he was going to be clean when he got to Ryker.

"Yeah. You do that," Ryker said. "I want a narc. Experienced street type. Undercover operator. Someone who can pass for a junkie or a pusher, knows the drug culture and the lingo. That's step one toward clearing this case."

SEVEN

Feeling hemmed in on all sides, Ryker left the precinct and walked to the park. He wanted to think about what his ex-wife had told him the night before. Somehow it didn't seem possible that she would marry again.

He chose a bench with only one bum lying on it, and rousted the ragged young man. "Get the fuck up and go to work," Ryker shouted at him, and the man, who was no more than twenty-five, rose slowly, growling, "Mother—" But one look at Ryker's eerie green eyes, and the bum shuffled off.

Ryker dusted off the bench and sat. He found himself staring at a curious structure: a miniature Greek temple overgrown with weeds and graffiti. Originally it was a drinking fountain donated by a San Francisco dentist who had struck it rich, not in other people's mouths, but in the gold fields of California. He built one in Washington, D.C., and another in Tompkins Square Park in the 1880s and dedicated both structures to the temperance movement. Unfortunately, cool, pure water as a replacement for demon rum just didn't cut it any better than just saying no to white powder. Reformers had the seeds of self-destruction built into their ideals, Ryker thought, and eventually they were revealed as fools.

He lit a cigar and tried to think of some kind of response to Eleanor's startling announcement. Did she actually expect him to fly to Chicago and attend her wedding? Maybe he should invite her to New York for her honeymoon. They could stay in his apartment. He laughed without humor. It made him uncomfortable to even have to think about Eleanor. She had always been there, or so it had seemed. He had loved her and she had deserted him and that had hurt him more than any other event in his life. But he had adjusted and grown used to her frequent calls: they made him feel part of something, necessary to someone—even if only tenuously. If she married, all that would stop.

Ryker closed his eyes for a moment, feeling strangely at peace, then thought about a girl he had once known. Her name was Virginia Bellardi, and she had been ten years older than the nineteen-year-old Ryker. He had used up gallons of hormones on that lady and was crushed when she announced she was getting married. He hadn't loved her, he would never have married her himself, but he couldn't stand the thought of her sleeping with another man. He didn't really want her, but he didn't want anyone else to have her either. That was the Bellardi Syndrome: he wanted all women he had slept with to revert to chastity after they stopped fucking him. Ryker knew it was crazy, but he couldn't help it.

THE SMACK MAN

He pitched the half-smoked cigar onto the park path and went back to work.

Three more junkies died before he knocked off around six. He hadn't bothered to go to the scene of any of the deaths, because he knew there would be more dead before long. The three dead junkies were all prostitutes and they all had pimps. One was found in her room in East Harlem, one was found naked in a cheap Times Square hotel where she'd just said goodbye to a john, and the last was a black girl found in a hallway in Harlem.

Preliminary reports from the medical examiner's office indicated deaths by strychnine poisoning in all three cases.

Ryker wondered how many cases had been reported and how many girls had been dumped into the river by panicky pimps. How many would rot in some cheap room until the stink forced someone to call the police? Ryker knew that all the dead were not accounted for and never would be.

The radio and TV news had finally picked up the story and were making a big thing over it. It had, after all, all the elements of a good story: sex, murder, and drugs.

All addicts admitted to hospitals for overdoses were routinely checked for strychnine poisoning now. A group called Addicts Rights of New York (ARNY) was formed by a Scarsdale lawyer and was sending angry telegrams and petitions to the mayor and police commissioner, complaining that junkie civil rights were being violated. A Baptist minister named Hinkley Epps and a lawyer named R. Vincent Stoneman were organizing a "Day of Outrage" for the

THE SMACK MAN

dead junkies. Heroin had suddenly become a racial issue, though most of the dead hookers were white.

All of these reactions from the media and the public had snowballed in just one day. Tomorrow would be much worse, Ryker thought. Tomorrow the slow-reacting politicians, especially those who had initials instead of first names, would start beating their drums and blowing their horns as soon as they figured out a way to grab some free publicity. Ryker had seen it all before. New York was a tinderbox waiting for a spark, a Third World city on the verge of tribal chaos.

On his way home to an empty apartment that night, Ryker ran into Chaos. Chaos was Peg's old man, a biker and a meth dealer who lived on the first floor of Ryker's building.

"Howzat' A.C. workin'?" Chaos asked.

"Like shit," Ryker said. He had paid Peg twenty dollars for it, and only constant threats kept it clanking along.

"You want I should beat the shit out of Peg?" Chaos asked. He seemed eager.

"No," Ryker said. "I want you should get out of my face."

The biker grinned, showing a checkerboard of green, furry teeth. It wasn't a pleasant sight. Neither were Chao's huge, rippling arms, enormous beer belly, and red bandana tied around his pointy head.

"Come on, Ryker," Chaos said. "I'll buy ya a brew."

"My life may be shit," Ryker said. "But I haven't sunk that low yet."

Chaos laughed. "You're okay, Ryker. For a pig."

THE SMACK MAN

For over an hour that night, Ryker sat in his living room trying to decide what to do about Eleanor and her fiancé. By midnight he was too hot and tired to think anymore; he was too full of Jack Daniel's to care. Women, he thought—but he didn't have a good tag line.

The morning air was already warm and moist as Ryker walked into the PDU squad room and began the long trek to his desk. Suddenly he became aware of a strange silence around him. He had an uneasy feeling that a lot of eyeballs were following him. He didn't usually say hello or goodbye to anyone, but the room had never become hushed when he walked through it before. He wondered if he was becoming paranoid.

Sitting in a straight-backed chair beside his desk, her back to him, was a woman. She turned her head slightly and he could see her profile. Late twenties, early thirties, maybe. He was puzzled. It was common for a detective to find a complainant sitting at his desk when he arrived in the morning. Good morning, I was raped. I was robbed. I was swindled. My car is gone, and so on. But there weren't too many complainants sitting around Ryker's desk in the morning. He was a supervisor; in theory, he was supposed to have people to handle the public for him.

Ryker approached his desk. The woman sitting in the chair heard him come creaky-shoed across the dirty linoleum. She rose and turned around. She was wearing a yellow miniskirt, a white Izod tennis shirt, and white Reeboks. Ryker looked her over. She was tall, at least 5'8", with long shoulder-length blond hair

THE SMACK MAN

and fair skin. Her eyes were green like his own; her mouth was a thin, tight line that didn't turn up when she smiled. It only got thinner. She was smiling now as Ryker stood directly in front of her.

"Sergeant Ryker? Hello, my name is Pamela York. Detective second grade. I'm your new partner." She stuck out her hand.

Ryker shook it mechanically, then walked around her to sit at his desk. He shuffled some papers on his desk and ignored her. Ryker had been prepared for a pimply-faced kid with long, punked-out hair or a thirty-year hairbag with a gut and uncontrollable flatulence, but he had never figured on a woman—a good-looking woman at that. For the second time in two days, he was incapacitated by a woman.

She cleared her throat and offered, "I've had plenty of undercover and street experience in Narcotics. I understand that was one of your requirements, wasn't it?" She received no answer so she went on. "I've been on the job nine years, the last three of them as a Narcotics detective. My citations include—"

Ryker held up his hand and stood. All eyes were on him as he made his way to Fischetti's cubicle. A lot of swivel chairs creaked as they turned toward the glass cage.

Fischetti was writing furiously on a piece of paper; his knuckles were white around his pen.

Ryker put his palms down flat and leaned over the desk. He didn't say anything, he just stared.

Fischetti looked up. His face was unreadable, but his eyes darted back and forth in pure panic. "Yes, Sergeant?" His voice betrayed a very small, nearly unnoticeable quiver.

Ryker began to mouth a word. He stopped. He

began again. "Is this your idea of a fucking joke, Lieutenant?"

"I beg your pardon?"

Ryker's voice was low. "Get that bitch gone. Now."

Fischetti's eyes darted away wildly from Ryker's dangerous gaze. The price of looking into those deep green eyes would be enormous. His mouth began to twitch; a tic developed under his right eye; his lips went white. He stuttered. "H-how da-dare you? I'll have your—"

Ryker slammed both hands on Fischetti's desk. Everything on the surface bounced.

Fischetti flinched. Then jumped up. He controlled his trembling voice. "Sergeant, either you go back to your desk and accept your new partner or you will learn the consequences."

Ryker pushed his nose closer to Fischetti. "You know fucking well that I don't have to work with anyone I don't want to."

Fischetti calmed down slightly. "That may be true if you find your partner incompetent, or if you have a personality clash, but it is not true if you refuse a partner because of age, race, or sex, Sergeant. That's called discrimination. Ever hear of it?"

Ryker was vaguely aware that discrimination was a very hot issue in the department these days.

Fischetti's smile was a sneer. "Several months will have to go by before you can prove incompetence," he said, moving to the door of his cubicle, meaning that the interview was over. "She may decide *you* are incompetent. Good day."

Ryker really didn't care if his new partner was a woman—or a Hispanic dwarf, a black hunchback, or an Irish lesbian. If they were competent, they were

THE SMACK MAN

fine with him. The problem was, he took chances. Many said he took too many chances. He wondered if he'd hesitate if his partner were female, and if in that one faltering moment, he'd kill her or himself.

"What the hell," he said, "she can't be any worse than some of the meatballs I've had over the years. At least she won't be bumming cigars off me."

"Don't be so sure about that," Fischetti said. He was a little suspicious. He smiled his all-is-forgiven-back-to-the-old-job smile. "Good. Well, you can show Detective York around and get her acquainted. I'm sure you'll get along famously."

"Yeah," Ryker said.

Ryker took the long walk back to his desk. His mind was racing—trying to stay ahead of the footsteps that were carrying him back to Pamela York. He reached his desk.

Several detectives watched him out of the corner of their eyes. They enjoyed seeing an old-time detective come face to face with the modern world. It was a giggle to watch the old guy squirm.

Still, many of them were jealous. Wouldn't it be nice to work late into the night with that piece of ass sitting at Ryker's desk? Surely such a close relationship had to end up in the sack. But since very few of them liked Ryker, they figured he got what he deserved. One or both of them would be standing in front of the chief of detectives with his or her heels locked together before the month was out.

Ryker sat down. His desk was in the rear of the squad room, out of earshot of the other detectives. "I'm sorry I kept you waiting," he said with a chilling smile.

"Quite all right." She crossed her long, smooth, tanned legs. "Did you get everything straightened out with Lieutenant Fischetti?"

"Oh, yes."

"So you have no objections to having a female partner?"

"Objections? *Me?* Not at all," Ryker said.

"Somehow you don't sound sincere," she said.

"Don't I?" He pulled out a cigar and leaned toward her. "Look, to tell you the truth, I want to dump you back to Narcotics so bad it hurts, but I can't. My ass is backed up against a fucking wall. Get it? Now if *you* go in there and tell that flaming asshole of a lieutenant that *you* don't want anything to do with *me,* I would be so grateful that I'd even buy you a beer."

"You don't scare me, Ryker," she said.

"Sergeant Ryker."

"You don't scare me, Sergeant Ryker. I've heard all about you and you don't scare me one fucking bit. Not one fucking eensy-teensy bit," she said.

Ryker lit his cigar and settled into his chair. "Okay, Detective York. Number one, I have no family. I work many, many hours. Long hours. That's no problem for an undercover cop, right?"

She nodded.

"During my long work day," Ryker continued, "I don't intend to change my work or play habits because of you."

"I don't care how, when, or where you get your jollies," York said.

Ryker blew out a cloud of smoke. "You any good with your hands? You know, hand to hand?"

"Enough to get by," she said. "Two big perps made

me as a cop once and I had them both disarmed and cuffed before my back-up team arrived. It's in my record."

"Yeah? You look like the type that would like to kick a man in the balls," Ryker said, waiting for her reaction.

"Do I? Well, it's part of the job. You know what happens when you're making a buy, and a bunch of creeps decide you might be a cop? They strip you and look for a gun or a badge or a body set. The first time it happened I had to pull my piece in order to save my ass. You know what my boss said after that? 'Don't wear a gun or a wire.' That's what he said."

She bit at a nail. "Have you seen the way these scumbags treat female junkies?" she continued. "Do you know the shit a woman has to go through to make a buy? Did you ever see how pimps treat their hookers? Have you seen the fat greasy bastards that run massage parlors? They treat those women like slaves. How about the demeaning, humiliating acts the women are forced to perform in the live sex shows? So if I have an urge to kick a few men in the balls, so what?" She glared at Ryker defiantly.

Ryker exhaled some smoke. "Takes two to tango, baby. I don't see any chains on those broads that you just mentioned."

She leaned forward. "The chains are there, *baby*. You just can't see them."

Ryker wondered if she was a lesbian. Well, what difference did it make? He was stuck with a very savvy bitch who had been around the bases and had a good idea of the score. He had to make the best of it. "You know anything about this case?" he asked her.

She nodded. "Yes, I was briefed late last night at

headquarters and again early this morning by Lieutenant Fischetti." She took out a cigarette.

"Well, I see a lot of busy beavers have been working late hours behind my back. Any ideas?" Ryker asked.

She lit her cigarette and recrossed her legs. "A few." She exhaled a stream of smoke.

"Care to share your ideas with me?" Ryker asked.

"Look, Sergeant, you have a rep as a get-things-done cop, but you probably don't know shit about junk. You think you do, but you don't." She began speaking rapidly. "I lived with it for three fucking years. That's why I wanted out. So what happens? My first homicide case has to do with junk. I swore I would never put on a pair of filthy jeans again and go undercover. I swore I would never walk barefoot through the dog shit and glass. I have medically induced railroad tracks up and down both thighs so that when a cock-sucking two-hundred-fifty-pound pusher says, 'Drop your drawers, sweetheart, I want to see your tracks,' I have something to show him besides my pink ass.

"I swore I'd leave all that crap behind me when I got out of Narcotics," she continued. "I burned my stinking street clothes and went to a hairdresser for the first time in three years. I spent a few days at the beach last week. I started putting antiseptic on my cuts and scratches instead of letting them fester. I brush my teeth regularly now. I wash my face and my pussy." She took a breath, then a drag on her cigarette.

"I'm very happy for you," Ryker said. "But all I asked was if you had any ideas." He was impressed despite himself. The two cops seemed to be groping for some sort of understanding. An armed truce. Green eyes met green eyes. It wasn't exactly love at first sight. In fact, it wasn't love at all. Only an admission by each of them that they would at least respect each other. They would work together until it was mutually convenient and possible to part company.

York bit her lip, then she began tapping her fingers on the desk. She began slowly. "What I'm saying is that from what I've heard of this case, the easiest, fastest, and probably the best way to trace that bad shit is for me to go back on the street."

"Good idea," Ryker said, knowing what it would cost her.

If she was waiting for something else, she didn't show it. "All right. I won't be much of a partner to you, then. But we'll make contact at pre-arranged times. I'm afraid I'll be doing most of the work. That won't offend your male ego, will it?"

"I don't give a shit if you do *all* of the work," he said. "I don't have much stomach for this case anyway, if you want to know the truth. Don't worry about my ego."

A little warning bell went off in her head. "What do you mean you don't have much stomach for this case?" she asked.

Ryker leaned forward across the desk. "I don't give a shit how many junkies end up DOA on strychnine. Or AIDS. Or any other fucking thing. That's what I mean."

She looked disturbed. "That's not very professional. I've lived with these people for three years. I think I understand them."

"You don't understand shit," Ryker said. The white truce flag was toilet paper again. "When you finally get your head out of the gutter, you'll realize you've been too close to it for too long. It's a common problem for undercover cops. You forget who you are and why you're there. You start to sympathize with the people you're out to bust. It's not unusual, and I'm sure you know it already. You have to step back from the problem. You're a cop again. You're not, nor were you ever, a goddamn social worker. Too many cops think they're goddamn social workers. You want to be a goddamn social worker, take the goddamn test for it. The first thing you got to understand is that the job doesn't require you to understand. Just bust the scum—don't understand them. They don't understand cops. Why should you understand *them?* Let the courts and the civil-liberties assholes understand them. They jump through their asses to understand criminals. Cops don't have to understand. Get it?"

Pamela York listened as Ryker put the finishing touches on his sociological thesis. She didn't agree with any of it, but she decided not to argue over it now. Maybe some other time. She wasn't used to social discourses on crime and punishment. Three years undercover had taken the sharp edges off her debating talent. Most street talk was a series of grunts, groans, and jargon.

"Maybe you're right," she said. "But we are not the judges and jury, too. If someone commits a homicide —junkie or not—as a professional it's my job to find that perp and bring him in."

Ryker looked out the window as though he was uninterested in the lecture, but it had hit home. "Let's not be in such a big hurry to round up this badass," he said. "Anyway, if we bring in this perp all legal-like, and we need a case for the D.A., then we have to show that, number one, we actually caught this guy selling heroin with strychnine in it and, two, prove in court that he knew there was strychnine in the junk and, three, that he put it there himself and, four, that he intended for the strychnine to be a fatal dose and not just a small cut and, five, that the already deceased victims actually purchased their shit from the alleged perpetrator. A lot of fucking work."

"That's what I'm here for," she said.

"And that's all I can promise you."

EIGHT

Ryker disappeared for the rest of the day, deciding to visit Beverly Kim's roommate, a high-priced call girl named Alice Sung. He thought that sex would cure his problems, but he was wrong. Alice, although a good technician, didn't satisfy him. He was looking for something he couldn't put into words.

Even his attempts at talking to the lovely, black-haired woman were rebuffed. It was obvious that he was a mercy booking for her friend, Beverly. Alice Sung had no sympathy for him and none for the street hookers who continued to die. "They are all terrible women," Alice told him. "They do not know the ways of love and are coarse—animals. They love heroin, not men." Ryker couldn't argue with her, but wondered about her own commitment to her profession. She was as cold as ice.

By 6 P.M., seven more junkies—all prostitutes—had died in the obscene arch-bowed position typical of strychnine.

THE SMACK MAN

By 6:01 P.M., three local TV stations went on the air with news about the deaths. All three stations broadcast appeals to junkies to go to methadone clinics. Many theories were bandied about over the airwaves by newsmen and so-called drug experts. One anchorman even hinted that it might be the police who were pumping the poisonous heroin into the pipeline. This caused an immediate uproar, and the statement was met by an angry, almost hysterical denial by the police commissioner at 8 P.M. But not one station bothered to carry his comments until the next morning. No one seemed to care about dead junkie whores except maybe the living junkie whores, pimps, mail-order ministers, minority politicians, and professional do-gooders. The mayor went on television the next morning and formally defended his police department and his police commissioner. Everyone who bothered to watch him concluded that by his strident demeanor and hollow-sounding words, he wasn't totally convinced that the police weren't in on it.

The TV people decided that they couldn't be bothered interrupting their game shows for messages from windy politicians. The many radio stations however, kept up a steady barrage of comments from DJ's, callers, and guests. By 10 A.M., four more junkie prostitutes were found dead, and the question then was, "Don't junkies listen to radio, see TV, or read the papers? Don't they know that there is dangerous junk out there?" Apparently a lot of them didn't. Or more likely, they didn't care. After all, tens of thousands of junkies *weren't* dying from bad stuff. When you need a fix, you need a fix. Period. If it kills you, who gives a shit?

THE SMACK MAN

At 10:30 P.M., Detective Sergeant Joe Ryker, by pre-arrangement, met Detective Pamela York near Tompkins Square Park. It was a Friday night, a clear summer evening, and the Lower East Side streets were crowded with bums, strollers, tourists, pimps, perverts, prostitutes, and crazies all looking to get off on something.

Pamela York was wearing a simple white dress. Her undercover life wouldn't begin again until Monday, and she was taking advantage of the opportunity to look like a normal person. Ryker greeted her coolly. This wasn't exactly a date. It was more of a walking tour.

"You're late," Ryker said.

"I had to meet someone earlier."

A man? A lover? Who cares? Ryker wondered briefly, then said, "I want you to meet Captain Kabbani and get acquainted with the neighborhood."

"I know both," she said.

Ryker shrugged. "You'll know more when we're done. Kabbani's the man to know at Borough Detectives. He thinks he's responsible for every bust in Manhattan, and I don't want him getting all bent out of shape because he wasn't informed about this undercover operation."

They walked silently through the hot evening, alert but unobtrusive. The last thing they wanted was to attract attention or see something that would require police action.

On East Fifth Street and Avenue A, Ryker took York by the arm and steered her to the Ukrainia, a bar that had survived virtually unchanged for almost a century: black-and-white tile floor, dark, carved wood paneling, copper ceiling, scarred bar, creaky bar stools, the smell of dirt, sweat, and beer. Ryker felt at home. It was the kind of neighborhood bar his father had taken him to when he had been a kid in Yorktown. While other kids learned how to throw a curve, Ryker developed a killer pool shot. He breathed deeply, taking it all in.

In a high-backed booth, at the rear of the bar, sat a short, squat man. His hands were hairy and his close-cropped black hair was flecked with gray. He had a perpetual five-o'clock shadow and a nose like a hawk. His friends called him the Camel Driver, and he was, in fact, Lebanese by descent. He wore a loud, striped suit that might have been used as a saddle blanket for a camel.

Ryker walked over to the booth and sat down across from him. Pamela York followed and slid in next to Ryker; they kept their distance from each other.

The Formica table was sloshy with beer suds. Ryker put his arms on the table, in the muck. "Nat, this is Detective Pamela York. York, this is Captain Najati Kabbani. Nat."

Kabbani gave Pamela York a good-natured smile. "Hello," he said, in a surprisingly soft voice.

"Hello to you," she said. "Your people picked me up for prostitution about six times when I worked this area. Every one of them was an illegal bust, too."

"Are you sure?" Kabbani asked, smiling.

"Very funny," York said.

"Nat," Ryker interrupted. "What we'd like is your cooperation. We need all the help we can get. We can—" A bartender came over and grumbled something about an order. Ryker picked up his wet sleeve. "You clean the motherfucking tables, Baldy, you might attract a better class of people. Bring us three mugs of that monkey piss you call beer."

The bartender made no move to wipe the table. He glowered at Ryker for a second, then decided that the man was dangerous and moved off.

Kabbani smiled, Buddhalike. "You've always been a politician, Ryker."

"That's why you love me, Nat," Ryker said. "That's why you're going to be cooperative."

"Haven't I always?" Kabbani said.

"No, not always," Ryker said. "York here will be at your mercy, and I don't want her hurt just because you've got a case of the ass at me or Fischetti. Got it?"

"What are you going to be doing?" Kabbani asked. He took a sip of his tepid beer, looking avuncular and benign. He wasn't. Kabbani was a shark who didn't differentiate between cop and perp when he was in a feeding frenzy. Ryker was wary.

"York here is going to go undercover," Ryker said.

Kabbani nodded and eyed Pamela York.

Ryker continued. "So as you know, this scumbag has been pushing bad shit around here heavier than any place else in the city. Half of the dead so far are from the immediate area. My precinct. What we'd like is some help. She'll pose as a junkie at first. That's her best role, I hear. Besides, she met a lot of street people in that role when she was here a while back." Ryker lit a cigar.

"Then one of my men, Williston, a black dude, will show her the light and recruit her into his stable. She'll take a bath, get real whore clothes and go back on the street. She'll turn a few tricks a day—"

Kabbani gave Ryker a sharp look.

"Not for real, of course," Ryker continued. "At least I don't think so. I've got enough headaches. But five or six cops a day will take her up to some fucking flea bag. We'll probably use Anti-Crime Squad cops for johns—type casting. That should satisfy the curiosity of the locals. Then she'll ask around for some extra smack. Look all strung out. Say her man's not giving her enough shit. She can do a convincing job of the junkie thing. I don't know about the hooker business, though." He turned to York, who was still smoking. "Can you handle the hooker business?"

"Why not?"

Ryker asked Kabbani, "What do you think?"

Kabbani swirled the suds around in his mug. He said to Pamela York, "You'll get picked up, of course. I mean, I can't put the word out *not* to pick you up. That's bad security for an undercover. You wouldn't want it anyway, right? So you'll ride in the wagon and you'll spend some nights in the slammer with a bunch of hookers. You'll even make the trip downtown once in a while to get arraigned."

"I told you," York said. "I've spent the night in your slammer as a hooker at least six times when your people scooped me up. I recognize you, by the way. You make lousy coffee." She smiled.

Kabbani looked at her curiously. Even his trained cop's eye couldn't separate her face from all the faces that had flowed past him on their way to Centre Street arraignment. He smiled back. "Okay. So long as you know." He shifted his gaze to Ryker. "There's absolutely no guarantee that this will work, you know. You'd have a much better chance just grilling the friends of the dead hookers. They might give you a lead on the pusher. Or maybe you should just wait for somebody to get busted with a nickel bag of strychnine. It's better than sending this little girl out in the street."

Ryker said, "If York wasn't such a lady, she'd tell you to shove the little-girl shit up your ass, you hook-nosed chauvinist pig. Anyway, there's more involved here than just tracing this junk to the pusher. Unfortunately, we have to have something for the D.A. Even you can understand that."

Kabbani nodded his head slowly. He knew what a motherfucker that could be. That's why ninety-nine percent of the prosses who were picked up were allowed to walk with a fine.

Ryker continued. "So we need a good solid buy. We have to follow this guy. We have to find his supply. Maybe we have to see him push it again after that. Maybe we even have to let a junkie die—although that's just between us, right? Anyway, we have a lot of shit to tie up before we make a collar and bundle this guy off to the D.A. So we need an MOF on the street. No way around it. That's not my rules."

Kabbani sucked on his lower lip. "Okay."

The bartender finally brought the beers. Ryker let York pay. The three cops slugged down the weak, warm foam.

"Well, can we count on your cooperation?" Ryker asked, draining the beer in one gulp. He felt he had sweated out twenty gallons during the last twelve hours.

Kabbani said, "My job's easy."

"Your job is not to fuck with the operation," Ryker said. "Just be cool."

"I suppose I can do that," Kabbani said.

"But will you?" York asked.

"What's in it for me?"

"No trouble from me, for one," Ryker said.

Kabbani laughed. "I guess that's worth something."

Ryker slid out from behind the table. "Thanks, Captain," he said. "If there is ever anything—"

"There will be," Kabbani said. "Believe me, there will be."

Outside, Ryker excused himself and called his ex-wife, Eleanor, from a phone booth.

"Oh, Joe," Eleanor said. "I'm so glad you called. I can't wait to see you tomorrow."

"I'm afraid you'll *have* to wait, Ellie," he said. "I can't make it tomorrow. That's why I called."

There was silence on the other end of the line; a truck rumbled by, spewing a cloud of noxious smoke. Ryker coughed. "Ellie?"

"I'm here," she said, at last.

"You okay?" he asked.

"I suppose it's my fault," she said. "I should have known."

"What?"

"That you'd never change, Joe. You can't stand to see me happy," she said.

"That's not true," Ryker said. "I want you to be happy, but I don't want to be your father and have this jerk ask my permission to marry you."

"That's not what I'm asking," she said.

"Sounds like it to me," Ryker said. "Live your own life, Ellie. Don't drag me back into it."

"Do you hate me so?" she asked in a small voice.

"Of course not," he said. "For God's sake, Ellie, I don't hate you. Never that."

"Joe, I—"

"Not now. I'll call you," Ryker said.

When he had hung up, Pamela York took his arm. "Everything all right?" she asked. "You don't look too good."

"Yeah? It must be the Bellardi Syndrome," he said. "You ready to go?"

NINE

Ryker and York walked east, then north until they stood in front of the red-brick Raymond Hotel. It had been built about the time of Ryker's precinct house, but was in even worse shape.

Ryker put his hands in his pockets and looked up at the old building. About half the windows were lit.

"The place only has about thirty-five rooms," he explained. "About half of them are SROs. Mentals, cripples, and old farts. The rest are used for what we once called illicit sexual congress. The owners of this place used to make a fortune on the traffic."

"No more?"

"Shit, there's more money in welfare warehousing," Ryker said. "The fucking business is in decline."

"These places give the precinct much trouble?" York asked.

"Naw, they keep a pretty low profile and we got more important things to do," Ryker said. "They keep things quiet. Usually the managers have some muscle around in case one of the johns gets crazy or something. Sometimes it's the hookers who get crazy. Try to cut and rob a drunk john."

Ryker was in his element when he was talking about this nether world that few people, even cops, knew about. Satisfied that he had a professionally appreciative audience, he continued. "Then there're places that differ from these fleabags in that they are the homes of hookers. The dormitories. The place where the pimps put the girls up. The stable. They offer cheap rent, are usually furnished, and the pimps don't have to put in a phone. The desk handles the messages. Cheap and efficient. These are usually a better class of hotel than the places where the girls flatback. Usually cleaner and more respectable than the trick joints. But sometimes a girl will take her john into a dormitory if he's afraid of the looks of the Larkin, Raymond, or the Center. You see?"

"You know your pussy business, Ryker," York said.

"Well, I just want to make sure you know your business—before you go around trying to impersonate a sidewalk hostess."

"You'd be surprised at what I know," York said.

"No, I wouldn't," Ryker said. "I just don't want to hear about it."

"I've lived on the streets and seen these people—pimps and hookers—but they just kind of existed on their own plane, while I existed on mine," York said, taking Ryker's arm. "Oh, sure, a lot of the junkies I knew turned tricks, but they weren't organized, you know?"

"Pimps are like a union?" Ryker asked. He liked and disliked the pressure of her arm.

THE SMACK MAN

"Exactly. You've got two kinds of girls on the street. Junkies who turn tricks and hookers who do junk," she said.

"There is a difference?" Ryker asked.

"Sure. Junkies are freer spirits."

"Sure," Ryker said. "Some fun."

"You learn to survive or you become part of the debris," York said.

They walked in silence until they reached the limits of the precinct, near Fourteenth Street, when York said, "All I'm trying to say is that I know the fucking score around here. For example, you know that bar there? The Elite Supper Club."

"Pimp heaven," Ryker said.

"Right. Let's go in."

"You kidding?" Ryker said.

"Nope. We might learn something."

"Like how to eat chitlin'?"

"Like how they feel about their girls copping fixes from an unauthorized supplier," York said.

Ryker shrugged.

Inside the seedy bar a juke box was blaring something that sounded like a cross between Tchaikovsky's *1812 Overture* and soul music. About a dozen black men sat in twos and threes around small tables. At least an equal number of teenage boys, hangers-on, and apprentices sat by themselves in the rear. The damn kids picked a sorry crew for hero worship, Ryker thought. But in the long run, maybe not. A few of the pimps had hookers with them. Three white bartenders wiped glasses and poured drinks.

Ryker walked over to the half-empty bar and pulled up a stool for York. A bartender hurried over. He looked big and Irish. He smiled. "Excuse me, folks, but I don't think you want to be stayin' here." He motioned with his head as though to say, "Can't you see all those bad-ass niggers, for Christ sake?"

Pamela York smiled a very upper-class, patronizing smile. "Oh. But we do want to stay. Tea at the Plaza is so terribly boring—don't you think? And all my crowd has heard about this quaint little place. We're all so anxious to have a little party here some night after the theatah. This is going to be the new 'in' place." She turned to Ryker. "Don't you think it's just so—so—real, darling?"

Ryker was embarrassed, but he said nothing.

York turned back to the bartender. "Give me a mug of that monkey piss you call beer, will you, please?" she said.

The bartender's eyes were growing wider. "Jaysus! Are you people crazy? Get out of here!" he whispered urgently.

A lot of eyes were staring now; the bar was quieter. Someone had pulled the plug on the giant screen video. This was serious business. Repel all boarders.

Ryker got tired of the game; in fact, he was tired of it before York began playing it. He picked up a bottle of long-neck Lone Star and smashed it on the bar. *"We are the motherfucking police, you assholes!* Can't you tell the motherfucking cops when you see the motherfucking cops! We want whiskey! *Whiskey! Now!"*

Pamela York pouted. "You're such a wet blanket. I was having a good time."

The bartender looked distraught. Panicky. He spun around and grabbed the first bottle his hand reached. He spun again and put it on the bar.

The crowd meanwhile had become restless. Groups

of angry black men were standing now, muttering in small groups. Many of them recognized Ryker now in the dim light. Ryker was pimp enemy number one.

The pimps moved into larger clusters like a coagulating oil slick.

York was pouring out four fingers of something called Georgia Moon Corn Liquor into a glass that had been left on the bar. "Such a wet blanket, Ryker," she repeated. She seemed oblivious to the fact that an ugly crowd had formed behind her back. She tossed back the short, squat glass of clear liquid. She looked very pretty in the long, flowing white dress, Ryker conceded grudgingly. The white dress, the blond hair, and her insouciant attitude were like a red flag to the pimps. They were not at all happy with this honky bitch or her cop buddy.

Ryker beat on the bar for another glass. The bartender quietly placed it on the bar and moved away from them. Far away.

Ryker and York kept their backs to the pimps, and drank the clear corn whiskey. "It tastes like paint thinner," Ryker said. "Want some more?"

York burped primly. "Yes."

Suddenly, a bottle hit the floor; Ryker spun around and said, "My friend here says you are the ugliest motherfuckers she's ever seen. Anybody want to argue with that?"

No answer from the grumbling mob.

"She also says that anybody who lives off a woman has got no balls and no pride. How about that?"

No answer.

"She goes on to say that the dumb pimps are losing all their hoors to bad skag and they can't do shit about it."

THE SMACK MAN

The angry crowd began moving like a black cloud toward the bar. They were between the bar and the exit.

"She further states that any time a black pimp sees a Sicilian, he takes off his hat, shuffles back a few feet and bows."

A tremendous black man, almost seven feet tall, stepped out of the crowd. He was dressed in a green satin tank top, high black Keds, electric-blue basketball trunks, and a black beret.

Ryker regarded him with a slightly bored look. "You some kind of basketball player?" Ryker asked, eyeing him.

The black man's voice sounded like it came from an echo chamber. "You might be the police, but you ain't immortal. Now you must want something besides botherin' the brothers. What you want?"

Ryker threw back another glass of corn liquor and lit a cigar. York kept her back to the crowd and kept on drinking.

Ryker blew a smoke ring. "Actually, I just wanted to get your attention."

The big man put his hands on his hips. "Whuffo?"

Ryker threw his glass on the floor. "I want some fucking answers here. I want to know why hookers are getting wasted all of a sudden. I want to know if you got into a scrap with the local Sicilian–American Social Club. I want to know how many prosses died and wound up in the river or the sewer. I want to know what you found out when you beat the shit out of your girls. I want to find the motherfucker who's poisoning the stuff. And so far nobody's come forward with any answers. I can't believe all you fucking people are deaf, dumb, or blind." Ryker puffed on his cigar.

THE SMACK MAN

The crowd began murmuring again. A skinny man in a blue chalk-stripe double-breasted jacket stepped up to Ryker. Ryker recognized him as a pimp called King Edward. "Okay, man, you want the score, but what you offerin' in return? You gonna give us that half-assed jive about bringin' this motherfucker to justice? Sheet, man, every dude here has been brought to justice at least ten times and we is still walkin' the road, man."

A laugh went up from the group.

King Edward had a pencil-thin moustache, and his sneering expression told Ryker what these people thought of the leniency of the courts. It was funny now that the shoe was on the other foot.

"So we got a real law-and-order group here, huh?" Ryker said. "A real motherfucking lynch mob getting set to grab into this badass and waste him. Well, shit, you got to find him first. And I don't think you gonna do it."

The giant with the beret spoke. "The brother asked you what you offerin' if we give you some shit, man. We wanna know what the blue pigs gonna promise this time for givin' some information. You always promisin'. Never deliverin'."

Ryker thought he saw a break in the solid wall of contempt and hate. A small opening. He decided to push it. "I'm promising you that I'm going to turn the screws on your ass so hard that there won't be a twat for sale for ten miles in any direction if you don't start being cooperative. I'm promising that if I don't get a lead tonight, I'm inactivating this fucking case until I do get some cooperation. I got a dozen other homicide cases in my book, and I really don't give a shit if I get this guy or not. Understand?"

THE SMACK MAN

The pimps looked at each other. They were caught between their instinctive hatred of the police and economic considerations.

Ryker could see that they were wavering. He decided to push a little more. "I got one lead myself and it points to your favorite Sicilian–American organization. Now there's some white ass we'd both like to see on the grill."

King Edward in the chalk-striped suit said, "You're wrong, man. We cool with them cats."

"The only people cool with them cats are lying on a slab uptown. They are very cool."

King Edward scratched his head. "We got a little somethin', man, but it don't point to that crowd. You jivin' me about the Mafia, man. That's just jive talk."

"I don't give a fuck if you believe me or not. And if I had my way, all your worthless hoors could DOA." Ryker stood to leave.

King Edward held up his hand. "Hold on, man. I'm gonna give you what we got. Just be cool."

Ryker leaned back against the bar. The situation was still tense and potentially explosive. Even as Ryker had gotten up to leave, he wondered how he was going to make it through the crowd.

King Edward spoke in his oily, impertinent voice. "Okay, man. We been talkin' and thinkin' about this shit. To your first question—we ain't stepped on nobody's toes lately, and I can't figure why we comin' in for this shit. We cool with the Mafia. They run the massage parlors and the porno shops and we run the girls. We even cool with the Muslims. We contribute to all these fine organizations—when they ask. We even give little donations to the Police Widow's Fund when we get shook down—I mean, asked." He

THE SMACK MAN

laughed like a snake hissing. The crowd laughed, too. Deep, resonant, and mocking.

King Edward continued. "Now your second question. Well, I gotta tell you—there's been a couple more prosses that wasted themselves on bad shit. Now some of the brothers get nervous and dump them. 'Specially after all the guff they gettin' when they do call the pigs."

He paused, stroking his thin moustache. "Now what we find out from our girls?" he said. "A white dude been tryin' to sell some of the girls nickel bags. And he's selling the shit for a twenty-five-percent discount. Right off you know something ain't right. Now, a couple of the girls done the right thing and went to their man and told him. A couple girls bought the shit and shot it. Nothing happened. Fine stuff. A couple girls got wasted. They all get the stuff from the same dude? Don't know. This the dude who poisoning the shit? Don't know. Could be, man."

Ryker dropped his cigar on the floor. "What's this guy look like?"

King Edward looked back at Ryker. "A white man with a beard, man. They all look alike to me."

The crowd laughed and hollered.

Ryker paid no attention. He fixed his cold green eyes on King Edward. "What color beard?"

King Edward's smile faded. He recognized the tone. He'd heard it before in a lot of fluorescent-lit squad rooms at three in the morning. "Black."

"How tall?"

"I don't know. Never saw him. Only the hoors."

"Fat? Skinny?"

"Skinny."

"Young? Old?"

THE SMACK MAN

"Young."

"Where's he hang?"

"Bitches spotted him from Harlem down to Chelsea."

"Name."

"Lots of street names, man."

"Give me some."

"Well, maybe it ain't the same dude."

"Try some names."

"Digger. Dr Pepper. Jessie."

"Why Digger?"

"Goes through garbage pails, I guess. Everybody goes through garbage pails gets called Digger."

"Dr Pepper because of the soda?"

"I guess so."

"Jessie? That may be his first name?"

"Don't think so. Nobody use their names on the street."

Ryker knew this. He fixed his eyes on King Edward. "What else?"

"That's all there is. There ain't no more."

Ryker looked around the room. Most of the faces were still hostile. "Okay. If you get anything else, the name's Ryker. Sixth Precinct."

"Hold on," King Edward said. "Now your end of the deal, man. No crackdown on the pussy. Okay? We cooperated."

Ryker nodded his head reluctantly.

"And you gonna work on the case and catch this motherfucker?" King Edward asked.

"If what you gave me is solid shit and not a tub of loose bullshit, I'll work on it," Ryker said.

King Edward held up his hand. "The motherfuckin' truth, man. No lie. Now what happen to this badass if you get him? He cops a plea for disorderly and takes six to a year. Right?"

The crowd laughed.

York was uneasy. She knew just how little fear of the law there was on the streets. It was a joke.

"I promise you everyone will be happy with the outcome," Ryker said, smashing his fist into his palm. "Very happy."

The words sounded like typical honky shit to the crowd, but the way Ryker said them had meaning. If Ryker weren't a cop, the meaning of those words would be perfectly clear, King Edward thought.

"I promise you if we find him first," King Edward said, "we gonna be very happy with the outcome. We gonna hit him upside the head with a brick, then we gonna take his honky head off with a fire ax. Yes, sir. We'll be very happy with that outcome."

"Where to now?" Pamela York asked, after they were safely outside.

"My Place," Ryker said.

"Not so fast, Ryker," she said. "I don't even know you."

"My Place," Ryker repeated. "It's what the pimps call a building downtown. About five years ago, some of the less dumb of them got together and bought a building. They use it as a crash pad—a place to get away from it all."

"An apartment building?"

"Yeah. Seven stories, fourteen apartments, heavy security. My Place," Ryker said.

"Why not?" she said. They walked a block in silence. Then she said, "I'm sorry I jumped to conclusions back there."

Ryker did not respond.

Fifteen minutes later, Ryker stopped in front of a nondescript apartment building. "My Place," he said.

"You ever bust their place?" York asked.

"Sometimes. But it's getting harder and harder to get a warrant. Actually most of the apartments are clean, anyway. They just live there. Someday we want to get together with the feds and the IRS and bust them for tax evasion. They can't show any visible means of support, but they live like kings up there. If you or I took an apartment in that building and bought an Eldorado, we'd have our ass in front of the Internal Affairs people so fast, your head would swim."

"Ain't it the truth," York said.

"Come on," Ryker said. "Let's walk."

"Not your place?" she asked, playfully.

"We got a ways to go yet," he said. "Much to talk about."

"Oh. I'm disappointed," she said, mockingly.

"Your ass will be dead if you don't listen," he said, taking her arm and urging her to walk faster.

"First off," he said, "you got to watch out for loony-toon hookers who'll cut you, your friends the junkies who'll rip you off, and pimps who want your bod in their stable. You should work it out so the Anti-Crime johns we're supplying will give you money and you leave it at the desk. Make sure everyone knows it, too. Have Williston pick it up. He can recycle it to the johns. Okay? Then there are wolf packs to avoid. They're college kids or high school fraternities or any group of adolescent males that travel in a group. They can give you a rough time. They're looking for a gang bang and if a whore refuses, they usually force her into it anyway. They're mostly just pimply kids from the suburbs, but together they have the balls of maybe one real man. Understand? Okay. What else? Yeah—" He hesitated. She looked at him expectantly.

"Yeah," he said. "The killing trick. Every year we get a few crazies who kill whores for kicks. Usually, they pretend to be johns. Not always, though. The prosses are prey for whatever crazy reason. Last year we had a nut who cut open their stomachs, pulled out their intestines, and took them home with him.

"So I have to tell you all this," Ryker continued. "Because being a pro is not an easy job. It's more than walking around with a meter clicking between your legs. You seen some things as a junkie, but sister, you ain't seen nothing 'til you seen the city through the eyes of a hooker."

York smiled brightly. "Sounds like fun."

"Yeah," Ryker said. "A million laughs."

As the two cops walked, they kept an eye out for a black-bearded white man who might be talking to the prosses for reasons of selling rather than buying.

They wandered in and out of the sidestreets, which were like so many sideshows, not saying anything, just enjoying a compatible silence.

Finally, Pamela York went into a long story about being down and out on the streets. Ryker couldn't help but think she must have partly enjoyed the degradation and degeneracy of being a junkie, make-believe or not. For even if the drug addiction was a sham, the filth and humiliation of day-to-day life on the street was not. He had trouble understanding her love of undercover work. He wondered what the fascination was with this type of assignment among younger cops and among women. He supposed that it gave them a chance to indulge in every type of fantasy—sexual, social, and moral—while at the same time acting as an agent of the law and getting paid for it. For surely in the back of the minds of undercover people, playing a debasing role, whether junkie, whore, pusher, gangster, political revolutionary, or rape decoy, must be the fact that somewhere there is a clean, safe haven waiting for them.

Ryker knew that a few female cops slept with criminals and revolutionaries as part of the job, and men, dressed in drag, enticed muggers and rapists. Narcs sold drugs. These were only a few of the suspect activities of undercover men and women, and he couldn't help wondering if there was a great secret buried under York's casual attitude. There were three years buried there—three years of urinating in alleyways, bumming off sailors and drunks, having her thighs inspected by pushers, sleeping with and maybe having sex with junkies and pushers, washing in public restrooms and asking strange women for sanitary napkins. All this not because it was strictly necessary—most of New York's undercovers went home every few days—but because she wanted to. Because she wanted to be so real and so convincing that even she couldn't remember sometimes whose side she was on. It was called total immersion and not many of the undercovers—drug, political, or criminal—practiced it.

Ryker interrupted a story she was telling about how she and two guys had once kept out of a snowstorm by riding the subways on free transfers for over three days. It was a real art not to get cornered into a non-transfer situation, she was explaining. Ryker stopped and pointed to a bar down the avenue. "Isn't that Woody's?" They had wandered back to the vicinity of My Place.

The sign was barely readable from this angle. "Yeah. That's it. Another pimp bar," Ryker said.

"Perfect," she agreed with a smile. "Let's go in." The smile said, "I guess I'm a little crazy." Her nostrils flared and her lips formed a straight smile. It wasn't the look of sexual complicity, but Ryker could tell that the look promised much.

"Is this a dare?" Ryker asked.

"Certainly not, Sergeant," she said.

"Well, if it's not, I'm going home. I've had it for one night," Ryker said.

"Aren't you going to ask me about your place again?" York said, almost coyly.

"Another dare?"

"Certainly not, Sergeant," she repeated. But her smile was wide and sensual.

TEN

Ryker slept alone that night, telling himself it was by choice. He missed the smell and feel of a woman in his bed; he missed Beverly Kim—hell, he even missed Eleanor Ryker. He drank himself into a Jack Daniel's stupor.

He awoke at 3:30 A.M., drenched in sweat and gasping for breath. At first he thought he was having a heart attack, but the pain in his chest was less severe than his hangover, so he sat up in bed and tried to get his brain to work. It dawned on him suddenly that the room was stifling. He tried to breathe, but it was like trying to inhale fumes from an oven.

Staggering out of bed, he smashed his toe into a chair and let loose a stream of profanity that would have ignited asbestos.

"Son of a fucking bitch!" he shouted at the chair and limped to the light switch. The air conditioner made a critical mistake at that moment by burping and humming. Enraged, Ryker seized the offending chair and hurled it at the window. The chair hit the upper half of the window, smashing out all six panes of glass and splintering the dry wood. It bounced back into the room, a leg ripping from the seat.

Ryker charged, grabbing the detached leg, and began to smash the air conditioner. It dented, but did not stop its ineffectual whine. Crazed with anger, Ryker picked up the straight-back chair and methodically rammed it against the recalcitrant air conditioner. Finally, the window frame cracked and the entire lower half of the window groaned and tumbled into the air shaft below. The air conditioner, its plug ripped from the wall, followed, hitting the concrete with a satisfying metallic thud.

Still raging, Ryker grabbed a Louisville Slugger he had once taken from a would-be mugger, and went looking for Peg, Chaos's old lady, the girl who had sold him the goddamn piece-of-shit air conditioner in the first place.

Dressed only in baggy boxer shorts, Ryker flung open the door and raced down the creaking wooden steps, oblivious to the stray nails that cut his bare feet. When he reached the first floor he smashed the bat against the flimsy wooden door and howled for Peg.

"Open the fucking door, you hoor bitch!" he yelled, smashing the door again.

Finally, Chaos, well over 400 pounds of him, filled the doorway, his hanging, sagging flesh white and disgusting in the dim light. "Wha' you wan'?" he asked groggily.

"Your fucking ol' lady ripped me off," Ryker shouted. "I want my money back."

"Huh?" Chaos was as smart as dirt; if his brain had

THE SMACK MAN

been as big as his belly, he'd have been a rocket scientist.

"My fucking twenty dollars, damn it," Ryker insisted, brandishing the baseball bat, wanting to drive it into the hanging mounds of flesh that draped Chaos like an ill-fitting suit.

"Go home, man," Chaos said, beginning to close the door. But Ryker wouldn't be denied. He smashed the bat into Chaos's toes, and the big man screamed. He tried to grab his foot to massage the pain, but he was too fat. He had to endure it.

"Peg!" Chaos yelled. "Get your ass out here!"

"Wha'?" a muffled voice from within the apartment said. "Wha'?" She was Chaos's intellectual equal, but not quite as good-looking as the bearded biker. Suddenly, Ryker hoped she was dressed. Fortunately she was.

Peg peered around Chaos's bulk. Her real name was Madeline, but everybody called her Peg because she had lost a leg in a motorcycle accident. Her doctor was sympathetic when he told her he had amputated her leg. The sympathy turned to shock when she shrugged and to revulsion when she asked for the leg to take home with her. She wanted to stuff it and mount it in the clubhouse of her Cycle Club.

Refusing to be fitted for a prosthesis, she had Chaos carve her a peg leg, and went tapping around on it like Blind Pew. Ryker liked her okay, but he didn't like getting ripped off.

"Damn it, Peg," he said. "That fucker you sold me wasn't worth shit. It fell out the window."

"I'll replace it," she said in a girlish voice. She was almost six feet tall with dirty blond hair and an even dirtier body covered with tattoos like her old man.

"By tomorrow, damn it," Ryker said, his rage subsided. He couldn't stay angry looking at Chaos's tattooed chest, a vast expanse that was dominated by a penis with wings searching for several fleeing—and dripping—vaginas.

On his way up the stairs, a door creaked open and a pinched face appeared. It was Sybil Fairweather, known as The Bat because she only came out at night.

"Everything all right?" she asked.

"You're the psychic, you tell me," Ryker said.

"Ah," she said.

Ryker had the sudden urge to moon her, but kept trudging up the stairs. The Bat had once helped him escape some badasses who were gunning for him, and he figured he owed her something, even if it was only preventing her from seeing his ass.

Back in his apartment, he showered and shaved and walked out into the sulfurous predawn. A hot breeze cooled, then made him sweat again.

On his way to the station house, a taxi stopped and disgorged a couple of punk kids, probably from the suburbs, Ryker thought. The boy and girl wore their hair in rainbow-colored spikes; they were tall, thin, painfully young, no more than seventeen, Ryker guessed. They looked ridiculous, he mused, but they must think they're beautiful. They snorffled up a spoonful each of cocaine, oblivious to everything and everyone, and went, arm in arm, downtown to the new club that had opened. Ryker shook his head and was thankful he didn't have children. He wondered how his own father would have reacted if he had shown up with rainbow hair. He knew the answer.

The precinct house was mercifully cool and quiet. Ryker went to the PDU squad room and spoke with the night-duty officer, signed in and devoted himself to some neglected paperwork.

"You're in early," Detective Callahan said, interrupting Ryker's concentration. "Come to see how the other half lives?"

Ryker didn't look up, but said, "Callahan, get your Irish butt out of my face and get me a cup of coffee."

Callahan laughed. "When you act like that, how can I refuse, Sarge?"

At 9 A.M. Saturday, Detective Pamela York arrived, apologizing for being late. "That corn liquor kind of wore me out," she said. "I hope I didn't say anything, uh, stupid."

"No," Ryker said. He knew what she was doing. She had had a few blasts, gotten sexy, and was now trying to pretend it was the liquor alone that had made her come on to him.

"Sit down," he said. "We have a lot to do."

They worked until six, then Ryker asked her for a drink at McGlade's, a cop bar near the precinct. She hesitated, then accepted after she made a cryptic phone call at another desk.

"This is about the assignments, right?" she said defensively as they were leaving. "I mean, I really didn't mean—"

"Why the fuck else would we go to a bar together?" Ryker asked, thinking of a few dozen other reasons. She was wearing a pair of skintight jeans and another one of those peculiar knit shirts with a reptile on the left breast. He was getting a hard-on just thinking about that beast and the breast underneath.

They walked together easily, covering the few blocks to McGlade's as if they had been going out together for months. He had to resist taking her hand, it seemed so natural.

McGlade's was crowded as usual, and as usual it was full of cops and cop groupies who exchanged sex or drinks for being a part of the Big Blue Machine. Normal people, civilians, found cops too loud, too rough, too dangerous, and too heavily armed to associate with in public. But the cops couldn't have cared less. They needed to let off steam—and occasionally sperm—before going home to the wife and kids in Jersey. They didn't seem to know that a few blocks away at the new club, their own kids were doing the same thing, only with drugs instead of alcohol.

He steered York to a table in the back, knowing they'd immediately become an item on the gossip hot line, but rather enjoying it.

They discussed the operation until well after midnight, then Ryker said, "Well, that's about it. What happens next?"

Pamela York smiled and said, "Are you trying to seduce me?"

"Yes," Ryker said.

"Well, it won't work," York said.

Ryker frowned and got up to leave.

"It won't work," she continued, "because I've already seduced you."

Ryker laughed and pulled her from her chair. He held her close. "My place?" he said.

"No pimp pads," she said. "Your house."

Ryker had managed to spring two of the three hooks on Pamela York's bra, when there was a tremendous crash outside his door. She had been soft and pliant in his arms, but at the sound she tensed, turning suddenly to stone.

"What the hell!" Ryker said, feeling his hard-on collapsing like a dynamited building. He untangled himself from York and went to the door.

Peg and Chaos were standing there, shit-eating grins on their faces; at their feet was an enormous cardboard carton.

"What do you assholes want?" Ryker asked, his voice a growl.

"We got your air conditioner," Peg said, proudly.

Ryker looked at the carton. It was an industrial air conditioner with enough BTU's to freeze meat. "You assholes," he said.

"It's a big one and it will only cost you a hundred," Chaos said.

"Eighty," Ryker said. "You owe me $20."

"A hundred and we'll install it," Chaos said, smiling his gap-tooth smile.

Ryker looked at the carton and shrugged. He doubted he could move it without help. "Okay. Come in," he said.

With a flurry of grunts, groans, and curses, Peg and Chaos wrestled the carton into the living room. York was looking at them as if they had suddenly descended from Mars.

"Where you want it?" Chaos asked, sweating and straining.

"Right here," Ryker said, indicating the living-room window. He hadn't had a chance to replace the bedroom window yet.

Peg used her wooden leg to punch open the carton,

and with Ryker's help, the three of them hoisted the huge machine into the open window. It fit. Kind of. Ryker had to shove a battered end table under it to hold its monstrous weight.

"Okay, everybody," Peg said, leaning over the controls. "Pick a temp."

"Cold," said Chaos.

"Fucking cold," said Ryker.

"Okay, plug her in," Peg said to Chaos. "Ready. Aim. Fire." She punched the "on" button, and a sound like a squadron of helicopters filled the room. Icy air blasted their sweaty bodies for almost fifteen seconds, then the lights blew.

"Shit," said Chaos.

"Fucking shit," said Ryker. "Where'd you get that thing?"

"It fell off a truck," Chaos said.

"Yeah, and it bounced a few times," Ryker said. "Where the fuck's the fuse box?"

"How about my hundred, man?" Chaos said.

"Oww," Peg shrieked in the dark. "You stepped on my foot, you big oaf."

"You're lucky I don't shoot both of you," Ryker said. "Get the hell out of here!"

"I want my money!"

"My fucking foot. I only got one good one!"

"Well, Ryker, it's been real," York said, edging her way toward the door. "Real weird."

"Come back," Ryker called to her. "We can start over."

"Somehow, I don't think this was meant to be," York said. "See you around." She walked to the door and left.

"How about fifty dollars?" Chaos whined.
"Oh, shut up," Ryker said.

By Monday, Pamela York had made the transformation into a flat-heeled, slung-shoulder-bag hooker. Detective Williston, with a federally confiscated, customized Eldorado, was trying to establish a reputation as a smart, mean and lean comer from Chicago. He would go through the motions of recruiting York, but he would soon find that the life of a black pimp was more public than private. On Tuesday he had to move into My Place in order to satisfy the insistent, "Where you live, man?" of his fellow pimps. If he had told them truthfully that he lived in St. Albans, out in suburban Queens, his stock would have plummeted as a Big Apple Main Man.

By the end of the week, through various means, Williston had acquired a real stable. One girl, a young junkie, begged him to take her on. He couldn't very well refuse and still keep his credibility with his rivals. So without waiting to get it cleared way up to the commissioner, he took her on and actually began to make money from her. So Detective Earl Williston was in the enviable position of being New York's only fully authorized police pimp. The money he made was put back into the Police Special Fund to pay for his apartment, clothes, gasoline, and spending money. The Special Fund was way ahead.

By the second week of the assignment, an older hooker, who belonged to a recently demised pimp, approached Williston outside a bar and asked him to be her man. After the first time, the second one was easy. He said yes. A third girl, who had left her pimp because he got a kick out of pouring boiling water over her in the bathtub, soon joined Williston's merry band. Williston looked big enough and mean enough to take her without worrying about her former man. So Williston began making himself or the Police Special Fund a lot of money a week. He was living high and enjoying the undercover assignment. His only fear was that Rodney or one of Rodney's girls would spot him and blow his cover.

Ryker was having problems of his own. He had called York twice on the Sunday after their disastrous date, but she had declined his repeated attempts to see her. He had been constantly on the phone with Eleanor, who had continued to call him, taunting him about her imminent wedding. The one bright spot in his life was, unbelievably, Chaos, who had found a fair-sized air conditioner for him—caught it as it fell from the truck—and had installed it. Ryker was cool, but the rest of his life seemed mired in the pits of hell.

On the job, he was encouraged to find that since the operation had begun, the poisonings had dropped dramatically. That was due, he supposed, to the mysterious "word" that somehow penetrated the dense minds and tangled subculture of the street. Still, thirty-seven hookers had died, officially; probably twice that many, counting the bodies that had been disposed of, unofficially.

The press had somehow gotten hold of some of the gruesome police photos of the wildly contorted naked bodies and spread them in the centerfolds with discreet blackout marks here and there.

The police commissioner was giving Fischetti a hard time about Williston being a pimp. Fischetti, at least, was true to his word and gave Ryker a free hand, shielding him from the nervous ravings of the brass. But it wouldn't last long.

Pamela York had been mugged once by a junkie, and almost gang-raped by a bunch of sailors. She had been scooped up by the pussy posse twice, which even Ryker had to admit was a pretty good batting average.

Of the last seven strychnine poisonings, Ryker had reason to believe that at least three were from heroin given to the girls by their pimps. It appeared that the pusher of bad junk was trying a new route. He had somehow gotten into the main line. Ryker suspected that soon the pimps themselves, at least the addicted ones, would start arching their backs and curling their toes. The manhunt for the skinny young man with the black beard continued.

Finally, by the beginning of the fourth week, a few days after Labor Day, Lieutenant Fischetti had had enough. He called Ryker into his office. Totten and Fernandez were there, waiting for him.

"Why do I let you talk me into these things?" he asked.

"Why not?" Ryker said. "Nobody else comes up with anything original around here. You got a better idea?" He looked around the small cubicle. Totten and Fernandez shook their heads. The absent Williston would have shaken his head, too.

Fischetti shook his head. "I've got one detective who turned pimp and another one who's turned whore and the P.C. is almost paralyzed with fear that the press will find out that Williston is running three real prosses. I wouldn't be surprised if he was running four real ones."

"What's that supposed to mean?" Ryker asked, tersely.

THE SMACK MAN

"You know."

"Tell me."

Fischetti wasn't sure he knew himself what he meant. He meant either that Pamela York was a whore or he meant that maybe Williston had recruited more girls and was pocketing the money. Maybe he meant both. He was a worried man. Very upset. "Forget it."

"I'll do that," Ryker said.

Fischetti was sorry he had said it. Ryker had that dangerous look in his eye. The lieutenant turned quickly to Totten, who was acting as a liaison with Narcotics. "They got anything over there?"

"Not a thing. They're really third-degreeing every pusher and junkie they get their hands on. All their undercover people are jumping through their asses trying to get a lead. They got lots of eyes and ears out there, but they can't get even a nibble. For a change it's not a matter of these people not wanting to cooperate—it's that they really don't know shit. This bad-dope guy is either very crafty or he has a big organization behind him. He's not your average pusher. He's slippery and he's smart. He's probably not really a pusher, either. This goes much deeper, I think."

Fischetti put his head into his hands. He looked harrassed. "He probably changes his profile. Different clothes, glasses, maybe even the beard and hair are fake. Maybe there's more than one guy."

"Don't take it so hard, Lieutenant," Ryker said, lighting a cigar. "Look on the bright side. Williston is happier than a pig in shit. Maybe York is, too. The Special Fund can send us all to Las Vegas by this time next month." Ryker blew smoke rings.

"You're not funny."

Ryker rubbed his chin. "What's more," he continued, ignoring Fischetti, "although nobody has the balls to say it, everyone is happy that the prostitution racket is in a shambles. Captain Kabbani will tell you the same thing if you pin him down." Ryker settled back and concentrated on his cigar.

Fernandez spoke. "This is true. Williston tells me this. He says the pimps are leaving the city. There is the rumor that the regular supply of junk has been contaminated with the poison. They say a pimp has DOA'd in his pad at My Place. His friends, they got rid of his body. Williston hears this."

Ryker sat up. "When did *you* hear this?"

"Just a few minutes ago. When he called in to me."

Ryker looked smug.

Fischetti didn't know if Ryker was playing the game to win. He wondered if taking him off the case would improve things. He decided to force the issue. "We have to end the covert part of this operation before it gets out of hand," he said. "I'm not even sure we're operating inside the law, having Williston running three real prosses—"

"Four," Fernandez interrupted.

"What!"

"Four. I forgot. What you say before. Reminds me. He says he got another one yesterday. He got a real stable now. A blonde, a redhead—"

"Stop! I don't care what he has," Fischetti said.

"That son of a bitch," Totten laughed. "That old motherfucker. He's never coming back to this here old station house. He's gone."

Fernandez laughed too.

Fischetti pounded on the desk. "Look, this operation is terminated as of this time next week. Ryker,

THE SMACK MAN

you are to make personal contact with York and Williston and inform them of same. I want a full report from them on their activities up until this point, a full accounting of what they've done." He pursed his thin, bloodless lips. "Where's York living these days?" he asked.

"Saxon Arms. But it's not cool to go there as a cop, and I can't go there as a john. It's only a dormitory."

"Well, where is she working, then?"

"In front of the Celite. I'll go there as a john, I guess. What do you want when I talk to her?" Ryker asked.

"Just tell her to step up her inquiries, and be prepared to terminate her activities by next Tuesday. A week from today."

Ryker nodded.

Fischetti expected more resistance. He was wary of Ryker. "And meet with Williston some place out of the area. Pick a bar on the West Side or something. When he calls in tomorrow noon, arrange a meet. Tell him the same thing and tell him also that he better make damn sure his nose is a hundred percent clean when it comes time to make a complete accounting of this operation."

"I don't think you have to worry about him, Lieutenant," Ryker said.

"I hope not," Fischetti said, unconvinced.

Ryker stood. "Well, I'm too horny to be sitting around here." He looked at his watch. "I should be York's first trick of the day."

ELEVEN

Ryker knew he couldn't pass for a businessman in his shabby tan poplin suit. He had to change his profile in case he was seen by someone who might know him, so he removed his brown tie and put on a blue windbreaker and a truck driver's billed cap. New York's delivery drivers were among the prostitutes' best daytime customers, which is probably why things didn't get delivered so fast in the Big Apple.

He put on a pair of cheap sunglasses and began walking toward Tompkins Square Park, then he turned south and walked down to Houston Street. South of Houston, he began spotting his first sidewalk hostesses. The glaring sun showed every wrinkle and imperfection in these dedicated career women, he noticed. Strange how he had passed them a thousand times in the last twenty years on the job, and he never thought of them as anything more than background props. His taste in women was more refined; he liked high-priced call girls, not street pros. Especially in this day of killer, sex-related diseases. You get what you pay for was his creed, and he didn't want to pay for his own death.

On the opposite side of the street was the Celite Hotel. He didn't see Pamela York. He continued past the deserted T & T Garage, called the twat and tit garage by the locals. A lot of the girls used the restroom there to freshen up. It was sort of a cooperative venture funded by three pimps who were simply squatters. No one knew who owned the property.

Ryker looked casually into the open door of the garage. He didn't see anyone inside, so he continued walking west on Houston. He crossed over to the north side of the street and began walking back east. He paused under the marquee of a porno theater and read the posters. Theater marquees were a favorite place for prosses to make a proposition to lingering men. As he stood there, a prostitute stepped under the marquee out of the sun. She was tall, about thirty-five years old, not bad-looking. She began reading the poster next to him. "I hear it's a good show," she said.

"Not enough nudity," Ryker commented without looking up.

The girl gave him a sidelong glance. She could usually smell a cop. She looked harder. Maybe. Maybe not. What the hell—you can't win if you don't play. She took a chance. "You wanna see a little nudity, big fella?"

Ryker shuffled his feet without looking up. "Gosh, I don't know. Where?"

She looked at him curiously. He didn't look like a man who would say "gosh." She figured he was putting her on. She said, "Down the street. That hotel down there. What do you say?"

"Sounds good. Sure."

"Come on."

"You go ahead. If I'm not there in ten minutes, start without me," Ryker said, walking away.

"You bastard!" She turned and stomped off.

Ryker started walking back toward the Celite. In front of Julio's Army & Navy Store he stopped and looked toward the hotel again. He saw her. She was coming out of the Celite with a trick. At least it was supposed to be a trick. Ryker imagined it was somebody from the Anti-Crime Squad. Still, it made him uneasy. The Bellardi Syndrome struck again, he thought.

The "john" was dressed in a blue sport jacket and slacks; he held a salesman's sample case. Pamela York nodded goodbye to him and began walking in Ryker's direction. She was wearing what the hookers called the little-girl outfit: penny loafers, knee socks, plaid pleated skirt and a white blouse; her shoulder bag was slung at her side. She wore a red ribbon in each of her two pigtails, but her makeup was heavier than a little girl would ever wear. Ryker thought the whole effect was grotesque.

She walked up to him and asked for a light. He lit her dangling cigarette. "How much?" he said, hardly moving his lips.

She gave him a funny look and turned around.

He followed her as she walked back to the Celite and up the steps. She stopped at the desk with her back still to him.

The clerk, a fat middle-aged man, looked at Ryker. "Want a room?"

"Sure." Ryker tried to sound nervous, inexperienced. He put money on the counter and accepted a key.

"Three-seventeen," the clerk said, for the girl's benefit.

The Celite required a registration card. Ryker hastily filled one out using the name Andrew Fischetti, his PDU commander.

When York heard the pen slide across the desk, she started up the stairs.

The clerk picked up the registration card and dropped a prophylactic on the counter and turned away. Ryker picked it up and followed Pamela York.

On the third floor, she turned around. "This way." She led him to 317.

Ryker put the key in the door and opened it slowly. He stepped into the room and looked around. York closed the door.

The room was like a silent movie set; scarred mahogany furniture and peeling flowered wallpaper. No air conditioner. It was about ninety degrees in the small enclosure. York opened the window and pulled the venetian blinds; dusty sunlight streaked in through the slats. The room looked out over Houston Street.

Ryker stood in the middle of the room; York sat on the sun-dappled bed. The silence was deafening.

Finally, she said, "The man I left here with a few minutes ago was Jonathan Shields of the Anti-Crime Squad. He talked about his wife and kids for twenty minutes."

"Is that so?" Ryker said. "I don't remember asking you who it was. In fact, I don't remember asking myself who it was." He wanted her more than he could ever remember wanting a woman.

THE SMACK MAN

"Okay. I just wanted to clear the air," she said.

"Consider it cleared. How did it go the last few days?"

"Not bad," she said. "A few hungry pimps gave me the most trouble. A lot of their hired help has disappeared in the last three weeks."

"At least thirty-seven to be exact," Ryker said. "Plus the girls who have deserted. Kabbani says that the number of hookers working the area has declined. A lot. I don't know where he gets those figures. Reminds me of those bird people from the Audubon Society that Totten told me about. They're screaming that the world's population of hummingbirds is down from eighty billion to seventy-two billion. How the hell do they know?"

Pamela York laughed softly.

"So, nobody approached you with any junk?" Ryker continued.

"No. But I'm trying to make contact without getting too pushy. I'm telling everyone my man isn't giving me enough and all that. The pimps here lost a lot of status on the street because of this thing. Still, not too many pushers are trying to sell to the prosses yet. The pimps are buying enough to keep them happy."

"How's Williston working out?" Ryker asked.

"He's having a ball." She laughed. "He told me he added a new girl to his stable."

"I heard."

"Anyway, he also said that he thinks that this strychnine pusher is selling directly to the pimps now or somehow getting the bad stuff into the pimps' supply line. There's a rumor that a pimp OD'd on strych."

"I heard that, too," Ryker said.

"Anyway, he's going to try to get permission to start scoring the stuff now. Maybe he'll score strych. He has to do it anyway because the rest of the pimps are always asking him where he gets his skag. And he has no answers. This way he can also try to make contact with the Digger-Dr Pepper-Jessie guy."

"Good idea," Ryker said.

"Do you think that's the guy we're looking for?"

"Could be," Ryker said. "Who knows? We get the information from pimps, who get it from hookers. Not what you call your usually reliable sources. Besides, there's more nicknames on the street than there are people. You know that. And how many bearded young guys with long black hair are there around here? Maybe a couple thousand. Besides that, if this guy did push the bad shit, he may have unknowingly copped it from somebody else. This strychnine poisoner guy may be using a line of intermediaries."

"I don't think so," York said. "If that was the case, the bad junk wouldn't only be winding up in prosses' thighs. It would be all over. It's been very selective."

Ryker shrugged, agreeing. He sat down on a wobbly, backless settee. "In point of fact," he said, "I just don't know. And I still don't much care. This is your only case, but I've got fifteen more in my book."

"What's this got to do with anything?" she asked.

Ryker stood up and walked across the small floor. "Well, I've come here to terminate your employment," he said.

"Meaning what?" she asked.

"We're sort of giving up for the time being."

"Why?"

"Why not?" he said. "The resources of the department are limited, they tell me. Anyway, we're only giving up the covert end of it. You and Williston are going back to the precinct."

"You'll never catch this guy any other way except undercover," York said. "Even if you do catch him, you said yourself it's going to be hard to hang a rap on him unless we make buys, observe him selling, see him—" her voice, on the verge of cracking with frustration, suddenly stopped filling the dingy room. He could sense her fury.

"It's not my decision," he said. "Although I have to admit I don't care either way. The narcs have the area covered." Ryker pulled out a cigar and lit it. "Maybe you want to go back to Narcotics and help them. Maybe they want to pick up this operation."

She stood up. "You're not getting rid of me that easily, Ryker."

"Sergeant Ryker," he said. "And who said anything about getting rid of you? We've had such a good relationship so far. I think it's called, 'out of sight—out of mind.'" He puffed on the cigar.

"That's not funny." She began pacing back and forth the short distance between the bed and the door. "This is not a narcotics operation. People were killed—therefore, it's homicide. The fact that they were murdered with drugs is incidental. Why do you get so goddamn panicky over undercover work? Jesus Christ. Bunch of old fucks in ripple-soled shoes. You all smell like cops. Spot you a mile away. Don't understand undercover work. Don't understand shit."

Ryker remained silent and let her get it all out. She stopped pacing. "How much time do we have?" she asked.

"This time next week," Ryker said. "That's pretty generous considering that the P.C. wakes up every night with screaming nightmares of Detective Williston being exposed as having the biggest stable of whores in the Free World—to say nothing of the nasty things they're saying about you in the squad locker room."

"I don't give a shit what they're saying about me," York said. "Any of those overgrown adolescents would give their month's pay to sleep with me, so what gives them the right to look down their noses at the kind of job I'm doing? Goddamn men. Are they looking down their noses at Williston, huh? He's not just *playing* the part of a pimp—he *is* a pimp, for Christ's sake." She was red with anger.

Ryker was sorry he had made the remark. He didn't feel like getting into a thing with her. He half wanted to take another dig at her, though. He wanted to inform her that some of the men didn't think she was altogether playing a part either. But he decided to let it slide. He really doubted that she was prostituting herself for money or kicks. He would have to crack some heads back at the precinct to make some other people see the same thing. But that might make things worse. There would be talk.

Maybe he should get some of the PDU detectives over here as johns so that they could get a better understanding of the operation, he thought. As it was, all of York's supposed johns were from the Anti-Crime Squad working out of the West Forty-seventh Street station house. They prowled the streets in assorted costumes, anyway, so they were a natural to be tapped for this job. Their usual job was to identify and apprehend muggers, rapists, armed robbers, and other violent criminals. Very occasionally, they got

THE SMACK MAN

involved with murder or narcotics. They were given a password for this assignment, and were told to approach Pamela York with it and proposition her sometime during their tour. In the event that a real john propositioned her, she had a couple of good excuses as to why she couldn't accommodate him at the moment.

The Anti-Crime men were also given a stern lecture about not trying to fuck her. So far, the locker-room talk in the Anti-Crime division was all complimentary. The men who had spent fifteen or twenty minutes with her had found her attractive and an intelligent conversationalist; they usually swapped undercover stories. The locker-room talk, as Ryker pointed out, was not so complimentary. The uniforms were the last holdouts in a changing police department. Most cops were married to very unliberated women and they expected all the women they came across to act the same way. The older members of the force thought the undercover women narcs were all whores. Ryker looked at York. "Forget it."

"Why should I? I have to work with these people eventually," she said.

"Before, you said you didn't give a—"

"I don't care what I said before."

Ryker shrugged.

She was getting worked up again. "Tell me—do they write my name and number on the men's-room walls, too? Pamela York. Good blow jobs."

"I did that," Ryker said seriously. "I'm sorry. I didn't think you'd mind. Good for business."

"Not funny."

Ryker stood up. "Don't let it bother you." He felt

curiously torn. On one hand, he wanted to needle her and get her riled up. Because she hadn't slept with him? he wondered. Was he trying to punish her? He shook off that thought. But while he wanted to get her mad, he also wanted to take her in his arms. For sex? Safety? He felt curiously protective of her, and he didn't like that feeling at all. Maybe that was why he was trying to anger her.

He looked at his watch. "We've been here long enough. I have to go back to the precinct and wash your name off the men's-room wall." He zipped his windbreaker. "By the way, Captain Kabbani says to say hello."

She was calming down. "Yeah," she said. "Hello to him, too." She went back to her thoughts.

"He was concerned that maybe his men were being too rough with you. None of them know who you are, of course."

She looked up. "They're okay. They're not a bad bunch for Vice Squad goons."

"I'll mention it to him," Ryker said.

"You can also mention to him not to look at me all moony-eyed like he does," she said. "All the girls say he's my boyfriend. He's going to blow my cover."

"I think he's a little in love with you," Ryker said.

"Just mention it to him," she said.

"You want to go downstairs together?" Ryker asked, eyeing the bed.

"No. I'll stay here for a few minutes," she said.

"Call me before noon tomorrow." He went to the door and opened it.

She called after him, "And get that concerned look off your face, please. You're supposed to look like you just got laid."

"I'll try," he said. "By the way, where does that junkie friend of yours work, the one that Williston recruited? I hear she's good-looking. I'd like to give her a toss."

"Sweezy Hotel," snapped Pamela York. "And I hope you get the crabs from her."

TWELVE

Ryker's next stop was the precinct house to wait for Williston's call. He wanted to arrange a meet as soon as possible.

His desk was littered with reports and phone messages, but what got to him more than anything was the sheer size of the case—thirty-seven murders. This was about the biggest case of mass murder he could recall, but because of the social status of the victims, and because of the nature of the murders and the fact that they were spaced over a period of time, the news media and public pressure were cooling. Consequently, the political pressure was cooling, too. There were lots of murders every week in New York City. Lots of big, juicy, revolting murders to capture the imaginations of gore-inured New Yorkers.

This morning, however, four more people had died. One was a small-time pimp. Two were hookers and one was a male junkie. It appeared to Ryker that the bad heroin was starting to diffuse into the general

THE SMACK MAN

junkie population. Ryker also wondered how much of the stuff there was around. How much heroin did the poisoner have access to? Forty-one dead.

Ryker knew that most of the world's heroin originated in the poppy fields of the so-called Golden Triangle, an area that included Laos, Thailand, and Burma. The poppies were harvested, refined, and shipped to Hong Kong by the Chinese triads—rich, ruthless gangs that made the Mafia look like Boy Scouts.

The Chinese White—the opium base from which heroin is made—was then further refined in thousands of home labs hidden in private Hong Kong apartments. This decentralized processing made it almost impossible to detect. Every *mama-san* had a kettle of opium boiling away; every skinny Chinese kid was a runner. More than a million packets of forty-seven-percent pure heroin slipped out of Hong Kong every day. *Every day.*

These packets were shipped all over the world to other criminal organizations—the Mafia, the Corsican underworld, the tongs, etc.—who stepped on the heroin and sold it to mid-level distributors, who in turn stepped on it again, and sold it to smaller and smaller units of distribution. Layer upon layer, Ryker thought, and all we ever see is the friendly streetcorner pusher, who was as far down from a triad as an amoeba is from man.

Asians, of all stripes and hues, controlled about seventy percent of the heroin business in New York City. But the current price was dropping and the purity going up on the wholesale level because the greedy Asians had flooded the market in an attempt to break the old-time organizations and drive them out

THE SMACK MAN

of business. It was textbook supply and demand that governed the price to the 250,000 New York City heroin addicts.

Crack had also cracked down on the power of the Italians and Asians, and had given rise to a new phenomena, the South American gangs. Ryker supposed that heroin had become an old man's drug, a relic of the past, while crack was hip, new, and in.

Ryker shrugged. Fuck 'em all, he thought.

The drug trade in New York was as shadowy as it was profitable. It was a billion-dollar business, and one of New York's biggest employers. Everyone, from little kids with beepers hustling crack to liberated sixties grandmothers, was in the business. And there was plenty of room for advancement, because there were a lot of sudden vacancies.

The spirited business competition among the Mafia, the Jamaicans, the South Americans, and the Asians had produced an orgy of violence. Importers, smugglers, wholesalers, cops on the pad, the DEA, the FBI, double agents on down to the local street-corner pusher—all became embroiled in the violence.

The sheer volume of the drug-related crimes paralyzed the police in some areas. So many of the deaths occurred in the ethnic neighborhoods that they rarely made the six-o'clock news unless they involved a middle-class white or an undercover cop.

The real danger for the city's drug dealers did not come from the law, of course, but from within their own structure. For all their undercovers and stoolies, the police were ineffective.

As the center of the nation's drug business, New York had become a place of murder and mayhem;

spurred on by official corruption, bad laws, an indifferent citizenry, and an overworked police force, heroin had become so commonplace as to disappear.

It was ironic, Ryker thought, that heroin had originally been hailed as a wonder drug. Its very name had been trademarked in the early twentieth century by the Bayer drug company, those wonderful folks who later introduced aspirin. It was first sold as a cough suppressant, and by all reports, worked very well. The one side effect, however, was a savage addiction, causing it to be repudiated by its Swiss manufacturers.

He rubbed his eyes, trying to grasp the enormity of the problem. It was impossible, and he didn't wonder that some private citizen had found his own final solution to the junk problem.

If that were true, this person, whoever he was, would eventually expand his operation as he became more secure and more trusted in the drug underground. This poison pusher was probably selling good stuff as a front, Ryker thought, though eventually he would tie into different markets somehow, somewhere, in the vast maze of the underground distribution system known as the pipeline.

Before 1 P.M., Ryker's theory was borne out. Three black schoolkids in Harlem had arched their backs in a deserted tenement doorway during their school lunch hour. The body count was now forty-four, with more to come. Soon after the six-o'clock news, the uproar would begin again. Ryker shook his head as he thought about all the trouble these new deaths were going to cause him. He considered asking off the case; he was sorry he ever asked on.

Williston called at 1:15. "How's it goin', Sarge? Where's Fernandez?"

"Jerking off in the bathroom," Ryker said. "I want to talk to you. Where are you?"

"In a phone booth at the corner of walk and don't walk. Uptown, near Broadway. What do you want to talk to me about?"

"Your expenses, asshole."

"I got to meet a dude named King Edward later on—business. Big deal. I don't know if I can squeeze you in, man," Williston said.

"Get your black ass over to McGlade's in an hour," Ryker said.

"How 'bout uptown for a change?" Williston asked. "P.J. Clarke's?"

Ryker agreed.

Williston was a good man, Ryker thought, and he didn't want to see his career go down the tubes over this assignment. He couldn't decide whether to talk Williston out of trying to stay on the assignment or to encourage him to buck Fischetti and the brass upstairs. He decided he'd make that decision when he met Williston face to face.

Ryker walked into Fischetti's office and sat down. The lieutenant looked up from his paperwork. "Can I help you?"

"I seriously fucking doubt it, but here goes anyway. I just spoke to Williston," Ryker said.

"And?"

"He's got a hot redhead lined up for you. He says you got to pay this time, though."

Fischetti looked back at his paperwork. "If there's something you wanted, get on with it, please. I'm busy."

"I was just wondering—does the fact that people other than prostitute junkies are dying now make any difference in the decision to terminate our undercover operation?"

"I'm not sure," Fischetti said, considering.

"Why not?"

"I haven't spoken to Chief Leidman or the P.C. yet."

Ryker shook his head in disgust. "I like the way you make snap decisions on your own, Lieutenant."

Fischetti was in no mood for Ryker's badgering. He rubbed his eyes. "I've been aware for some time that you don't like the way I've been running this PDU and quite frankly, I don't give a damn."

Ryker pulled out a cigar. "Is that so? Listen, I didn't come in here to bump heads. After today, I want out."

Fischetti looked pleased. "Presto chango—you're out. So's York. So's Williston. We're going back to regular police methods next week if not sooner. This pimp-pross garbage has gotten us nowhere. It might land us all in jail if we're not careful." Fischetti leaned back in his chair. "Have you arranged to meet Williston yet?"

"Yeah." Ryker got up.

Before he left the office, Ryker called Beverly Kim, who was back from Europe. He hoped to hell they could resume their off-and-on life together, for although she was a high-priced party girl, Beverly had taken a liking to Ryker. They had something going beyond a supplier-consumer relationship. Ryker recognized in her a toughness that matched his own—a toughness he had found recently in Pamela York.

"Ryker!" Beverly said into the phone.

"Hiya, babe. Good trip?"

"The best," she said. "But I'm glad to be back."

"I'm glad, too," he said. "How about a reunion, ten P.M. tonight?"

"Sure, if I don't have a date," she said.

"You got one," he said. "Me."

"You paying?"

"You kidding?" he said. Ten large was a bit steep for a cop, even if he was a sergeant.

"Well, it *has* been a while," Beverly said. "I'll clear my calendar for you tonight. Your place?"

"Yep."

"Is it a wreck?"

"Last person to clean it up was you," Ryker said. "But I got a new air conditioner."

"Too bad," she said. "I was looking forward to licking the sweat off your balls."

"Me, too," Ryker said, hanging up.

Ryker took a cab to Fifty-fifth Street and Third Avenue. It had been months since he had been uptown. The trip was little more than two miles, but it was a very long distance on the tight little island of Manhattan.

Ryker glanced at the chic restaurants and singles pubs as he walked around for a moment. Most of the people he passed were better-dressed, better-looking, and snottier than the locals in the East Village. They made Ryker sick. He knew what they really were. Effete. Degenerate. Snobbish. Weak. He'd had dealings with them before.

He watched a lot of young girls pass by. They looked sharp, but Ryker knew the pathetic lives most of them led. He was sure they didn't think of themselves as pathetic, however. Most of them were originally from out of town, had come to the Big Apple and had settled in the East Side girl ghetto for two reasons: an exciting career or to meet Mr. Right. They usually wound up as receptionists or secretaries and the guys they woke up next to week after week turned out to be Mr. Wrong. They lived too many in too few rooms for which they paid too much rent.

East Side. West Side. Lower East Side. Upper West Side. Harlem, Spanish Harlem. The Bowery. Greenwich Village. Chinatown. Little Italy. Chelsea. Ryker had worked them all. The thing they all had in common was the pervasive fear of the residents. Ryker's thoughts were that they should just be done with it, and elect a murderer as mayor, an embezzler as controller, a rapist as district attorney, and a mugger as police commissioner. Maybe a junkie thrown in as assistant mayor. Just be done with it and make it official. Ryker smiled at the thought. What difference did it make, though? New York would always be New York. The eternal city, like Rome. No matter how many Vandals and Huns overran its streets, its massive buildings and monuments would stand tall and attract yet more and more would-be emperors, kings, and popes who would all promise to save her. No one would succeed, yet no one would fail. The city would just go on.

Ryker approached the small, three-story brick building that housed P. J. Clarke's. The nineteenth-century structure was dwarfed by the immense office buildings that rose on Third Avenue. The fact that P. J.'s was one of the last of the old structures in the area that hadn't fallen before the wrecker's ball gave it perhaps more charm than it deserved. More charm

THE SMACK MAN

than if it were located next to other nineteenth-century buildings in the Village or Chelsea or Brooklyn Heights.

The patrons cascaded down the elevators of the surrounding steel-and-glass high-rises, streamed through the door of the place and settled into the authentic last-century decor. The bar, as always, was jammed and the patrons drank martinis, beer, and fuzzy navels as though the wrecker's ball was just a parabolic swing away.

The floor was ceramic-tiled and the ceiling pressed zinc; the wood bar was dark, the mirrors paneled, etched, and curved. The customers sometimes got drunk, but they were orderly. The place had an Irish flavor, as its name implied, but all type and manner of people called it home. It was the bar in Ray Milland's famous movie, *Lost Weekend*.

Ryker pushed through the wood and glass door. It was 2:30 P.M.

He scanned the bar for Williston, then passed through the long barroom and looked into the restaurant. No luck. He walked back over to the bar, sidled through a crack in a group of businessmen discussing the merits of pussy, and ordered a Jack Daniel's. The bartender dumped a prim amount into the glass. Ryker ordered a double.

At 2:50 he began wondering if Williston had decided to meet King Edward first. At 3:10, after a second double, he began to worry. At 3:30, he was pretty sure that Williston was dead. Ryker couldn't imagine anything that would keep Williston from a meeting with him except a stopped heart. He made a phone call to the station house; they hadn't heard from the cop turned pimp.

THE SMACK MAN

Ryker walked outside and thirty minutes later he was in front of Williston's city-financed apartment in My Place. He flashed his tin at a surprised and angry doorman and got into the elevator. On the way up, he wondered if he should have called the precinct again. He decided to wait and see what he found.

Ryker got off on the fifth floor and walked to apartment 5-C, but before he could even speculate about what was behind the door, he knew.

Ryker stared into a small round hole that shouldn't have been there where the peephole was. A cool stream of air conditioning hit him in the face as he stared blankly at the hole. A ring of gunpowder discolored the tan door.

Ryker walked slowly and mechanically to the wall opposite the door. There was no hurry now. He pushed off from the wall and kicked. The door jamb splintered. He kicked again and again. Two of the three locks on the door crunched, snapped, and sprung. The door was loose from the jamb, but wouldn't swing inward freely. Ryker realized why. He slid into the foot-wide opening and closed the door.

Sprawled out, arms and legs askew, was Earl Williston. He had apparently been changing from his pimp threads into something more suitable for his meet with Ryker when he had answered the ring at the door. He was dressed in lavender silk boxer shorts and a lavender silk T-shirt. He had a good sense of detail, Ryker reflected. Who else would have thought of wearing pimp-type underwear?

A large-caliber bullet had entered through Williston's right eye as he pressed it against the peephole. The pressure from the bullet inside the cranium had caused the skull to split above the right ear. What Ryker could see of the back of the head looked like it had exploded. There were flecks of brain and clots of blood on the dead cop's shoulder and face. The floor was splattered with gray and red; pink and white flesh showed through the black skin. At least it had been very quick, Ryker thought. A bullet in the brain had to be quick, he told himself. The face showed no pain. . . .

Someone was pounding on the door behind him, he realized suddenly, and he turned around to pull the door open as much as Williston's feet and legs would allow. He also pulled his gun. Six black men, dressed in outrageous flash clothes, stood there like a citizens' committee waiting for some answers.

"Police business!" he bellowed. "Nobody move!"

A few sets of hands went up tentatively. You see a gun, you put your hands up, was the rule followed by many New Yorkers. Cop gun. Criminal gun. What difference did it make? Two men went for their own pieces.

"You're all fucking witnesses! Everyone of you motherfuckers is a witness." He wondered why he was screaming. His head was spinning. He'd seen enough dead bodies to fill a good-sized swimming pool, but when a cop got it, he suddenly became aware of his own mortality again. "You!" He pointed his gun at a frightened-looking man in an orange suit. "You! Call the police, you fuck! Now! Now!"

The man ran down the hall.

Ryker leaned against the splintered door jamb. He felt shaky and enraged at the same time. He was barely aware that the crowd had vanished.

Ryker wiped the sweat off his upper lip. He wondered who had made Williston. Maybe nobody made him for a cop. Maybe a pimp just killed him for some kind of pimp reason. Maybe one of his girls. Could have been anybody, he decided. When you go underground in the underworld, you are automatically on a lot of shit lists.

The police came. A patrolman with two rookie cops. Ryker made a short concise statement and left. He didn't want to be around when Fischetti arrived. He had a lot to do before the long, restraining arm of officialdom caught up with him. For the first time in weeks he felt motivated. And when he felt motivated, he felt mean. And when he felt mean, he liked to bust skulls.

The desk clerk at the Henry Hudson Hotel, where Rodney was living, said that he hadn't seen the pimp all day, but he thought Rodney might still be in his room because he usually slept until four or five.

Ryker knew that a pimp's day usually began with breakfast about four P.M. He could believe that Rodney was still in his room at this hour. But if he were in his room, he didn't kill Williston even though he had the time to do it. You just don't kill a cop in New York without changing your address. Ryker took a passkey from the clerk and got on the elevator.

Outside of Rodney's door, Ryker listened quietly for a few seconds; he heard nothing. With the passkey, he quietly unlocked the door and pushed it open. A chain held the door open three inches. Rodney was asleep in his bed. Ryker hit the door with his shoulder and snapped the chain. He stepped inside and closed the door behind him.

Rodney awoke with a start and began fumbling under his pillow. As the sleep cleared from his eyes, he realized that it was Ryker standing like a bad dream at the foot of the bed. He smiled sleepily as he patted at the pillow as though he were fluffing it up. He didn't want Ryker to get some crazy idea that he had a gun under that pillow. He fluffed the pillow a few more times for Ryker's benefit and smiled again. "What's happening?"

Ryker launched himself like a broad jumper, and landed full length on Rodney. Rodney made a noise like a high-speed blowout.

Ryker's two big fists came down simultaneously on either side of the pimp's head. Rodney's eyes bulged and his tongue shot out. Ryker knelt with his two hundred and twenty pounds on Rodney's chest. He started destroying the pimp's face with his powerful fists. When he figured he'd pulped every area of Rodney's face, he stopped. He dug his knees into the pimp's narrow chest.

Ryker knew that Rodney didn't kill Williston, but there was still the possibility that he knew who did. This was just Ryker's way of getting the pimp's attention before he started asking him questions and getting nasty with him. *"You hear me, motherfucker? You hear me?"*

Rodney, who had been sleeping so peacefully only seconds before, heard very little. He was stunned.

Ryker slapped him across the face a few times. *"Wake up, you cocksucker!"*

Rodney nodded his head. His eyes opened, but rolled back and closed again.

Ryker wondered if he had hit him a little too hard. He grabbed a pint of peach schnapps from the night table and poured half of it on Rodney's face. He poured some between Rodney's slack lips. Rodney swallowed automatically, then gagged some up.

Ryker drank some of it himself while he waited for Rodney to respond. It tasted like rotten fruit.

Ryker poured the rest of the schnapps through his waiting lips. "Now listen to me, shithead, and pay attention." Ryker hit him gently between the eyes with the bottle. "You awake?"

Rodney nodded his bloody head, slowly.

"You remember Williston? You remember the black detective that took your statement in your apartment?"

Rodney nodded.

"You ever see him again?"

Rodney shook his head.

Ryker raised the bottle.

Rodney shook his head violently.

"Never?"

"Neber," through swelling lips. "Please." The words were soft and bloody-bubbly.

"You ever hear of a pimp called Lord Earl?"

Rodney nodded affirmatively.

"You know him good, asshole?"

"No, man. No." He shook his head half to reinforce the negative reply, half to try to clear his numbed brain.

"You ever see him around?"

"No."

"How the fuck could you know about him and never see him, you lying motherfucker?"

"Neber seen him, man. Hearda da dude, man." Rodney's lips and face were becoming puffy. "From Chicago."

THE SMACK MAN

Ryker had to believe him. Rodney wasn't made out of the kind of stuff that could take a beating like this without cracking. "You know a pimp called King Edward?"

Rodney nodded.

"Where's he live?"

"My Place."

Ryker knew he should have checked it out when he was there, but his first reaction was to get his hands on Rodney. "Where's your girls now, you prick? Where are they, shithead?"

"Here. Here. Same place. 1217. Only three left. Please, man. Back off. Why this happen to me? Why?"

"You're scum, Rodney," Ryker said. "And I'm a scum magnet." Ryker shoved his hand under Rodney's pillow and extracted a snub-nosed Smith and Wesson .38, and stuck it in his belt. "We were meant for each other."

The two sweating men both sucked in air for a few seconds. Ryker rolled off the bed and began ripping through Rodney's things. He found nothing interesting and left.

On the other side of the Henry Hudson Hotel, and two floors up, he stood in front of one of the doors of the adjoining suites. Suite 1217. He knocked softly.

"Who's there?" A cheery, feminine voice.

"Joe Ryker, ma'am. Police Department. I spoke to you about Vivien and Nancy last month. Remember?"

The prostitute remembered. She was the one who Ryker had interrupted at the Sweezey Hotel. But his pleasant-sounding voice didn't fit the image of the man she remembered so well—the man who had come crashing through the door like a bulldozer. She

THE SMACK MAN

peeped through the peephole, saw the upheld badge, and opened the door.

It was him all right. If she had any doubts about that, they were quickly put to rest when he punched her in the stomach. She doubled over and sunk to her knees.

Ryker closed the door and strode into the room. He looked around. One of the girls was in bed reading a movie magazine. The other was apparently taking a shower; he could hear the water running in the bathroom through the half-open door.

The girl in the bed dropped her magazine and sat up, wide-eyed. She looked back and forth between Ryker and her girlfriend on the floor fighting for breath.

The girl on the floor was crawling around aimlessly, trying to breathe. Her robe had fallen open and her big breasts hung down.

Ryker walked over to the bed and grabbed the terrified girl by the front of her frilly teddy. With one hand he yanked her out of bed and threw her across the room. She bounced off the wall and fell to the floor beside the other girl.

Ryker looked down at the pair. "Stay there. If you move one inch, I'll kill you." He walked into the other room and came back with a dripping wet blonde, whom he didn't recognize. New meat. He held her by the hair like a kewpie doll, and spun her around so that she faced him. The other two girls huddled together on the floor. Ryker released his grip on the blonde's hair and she fell to her knees in front of him. Instinctively she grabbed his legs for support; he pulled her head back by the hair.

The blonde had been beaten many times before, by

THE SMACK MAN

a series of men, but usually she had the small satisfaction of knowing why. This time she didn't even know *who*. The other two girls huddled closer to each other.

Ryker looked at them. Then at the girl at his feet. "You know Lord Earl?"

The question cleared the air right away. The girls now knew that he wanted information. Regular cop stuff. For a while they thought that maybe he just got his jollies beating whores. They thought maybe they were going to get paid for the beatings. They'd all done that trick before.

The girl who had been lying in bed reading, Elaine, spoke up timidly. "We know him. We seen him around."

Ryker let the blonde slip to the floor. He sat on the bed. "Okay. Tell me all about Lord Earl."

They told him. They practically fell all over each other telling him. They interrupted and corrected each other. They spoke in small excited voices as though the faster they spoke the better the chance they had to keep Ryker on the bed.

Ryker listened and asked questions. Lord Earl was a new pimp from Chicago, they told him. He had a reputation of being tough but fair with his girls. He had become a sort of folk hero among the prosses in the short time he had set up shop. The girls held him up as an example of what a man should be like. Did the pimps dislike him, then? Was there a pimp vendetta against him? No. He was respected, if not liked, by the rest of the pimps. He was intelligent. He seemed to know the law well. He helped a lot of the brothers out of tight scrapes with the police. He bought a lot of drinks for everyone. The men might have thought he was a little too well-mannered and that he treated all his girls too well, but he had a tough streak in him. He never stepped on anyone's toes and got along with all types of street people. Besides, he carried a big gun and wasn't afraid to flash it around.

Ryker got up. There was not even a hint in what they said that someone had made Williston as a cop. As far as anyone knew, he was Lord Earl. The big, black Eldorado-mounted knight. Then who made him and who burned him?

King Edward was next on his list.

THIRTEEN

My Place was surrounded by police, now. Squad cars and barricades lined the streets and sidewalks. It was obvious from the number of police that the Midtown South was taking advantage of Williston's murder to rip the place apart.

Ryker held up his badge and walked through the barricades. Suspects and witnesses lined the walls. Everyone was screaming at everyone else. He noticed that the police were being particularly nasty. So were the pimps.

Ryker didn't see King Edward in the lobby, but he did see Fischetti. Ryker stepped behind a pillar and waited for a chance to get to the elevator bank.

Fischetti and some of the other detectives from his PDU were grilling a group of tenants. Ryker spotted Fernandez. It appeared as though the usually happy detective had been crying.

As Ryker moved into the elevator, he found himself standing next to a wheeled stretcher. An assistant medical examiner and three orderlies stood at the four corners of the blood-splattered sheet covering the body. They wheeled Williston into the lobby. Ryker pushed a button at random.

Sixth floor. As good as any. There was no directory in the building and everybody had a lot of names anyway. All Ryker knew was that Williston had had an appointment with King Edward, and when he found King Edward, the pimp would tell him all about it. Ryker wondered if Williston had broken the appointment or had gotten it over with before he was to meet Ryker. And would King Edward, who lived at My Place and who knew Williston, and who had an appointment with him, have to shoot him through a peephole? Not likely. But there wasn't much else to go on.

The elevator stopped on the sixth floor. In the hall, a lot of uniformed policemen and detectives were taking statements from unhappy-looking people. Some of the detectives recognized Ryker and nodded. One informed him that his lieutenant was looking for him. Ryker walked through the halls, asking questions, then he tried different floors. He learned that King Edward was somewhere in the building. Some apartment doors were open and vigorous apartment searches were in progress or had been completed. Odd pieces of furniture and bits of clothing lay scattered in the halls. Several people were being led to the elevators in handcuffs, probably on dope and gun charges, Ryker thought. He doubted if the charges would stick, given the rules of search, but it would cost the tenants some time and money, anyway. Midtown South was definitely taking out a lot of frustration on My Place now. The death of a cop made everyone a little crazy, Ryker thought. A whole apartment building was being shaken down like it was a broom closet. Blue uniforms burrowed in and out like so many ferrets. In its wake, today's operation would leave a pile of complaints on the desk of the Civilian Complaint Review Board. A trash can full of angry messages from the Civil Liberties Union would wind up on the commissioner's desk. There would be a floor covered with hair from the head of the mayor, who couldn't afford the loss, and hysterical telephone messages from his office to the police commissioner, who would try frantically to keep sitting on the fence between the cops and the politicians.

The cops involved would counter with a lot of search warrants which had probably not even been issued yet, and a string of angry denials about abridgement of anyone's civil rights. They would pose in front of news cameras with tables full of weapons, dope, and drug paraphernalia.

As usual, everyone would be a little right and a little wrong at the same time. Ryker shrugged. What difference did it make? What difference did it make to Williston, or his widow and two kids in St. Albans?

If you really needed information and you were going to step outside the law a little and search someone's apartment without a proper warrant, or question someone even though he demands to be represented by counsel, then you might as well go all the way and beat the shit out of him, Ryker thought. You might as well face a departmental trial for a big no-no as for a little one. At least you got results with the big ones.

He found King Edward talking to a uniformed

patrolman on the second floor. Ryker took the pimp down the hall to his apartment.

Ryker looked around inside the pimp pad. It had already been turned over. The expensive velvet furniture was upside down and the chrome and glass accessories lay scattered about like industrial waste on a factory floor.

King Edward stood in the middle of his living room and looked at Ryker warily. He remembered him from the bar, so he began carefully. "Look what they done—"

"Shut your fucking mouth!" Ryker turned on him. "You had an appointment with Lord Earl this afternoon. Right?"

The pimp looked surprised for a second. Only two people in the world knew that; one of them was dead and the other was himself. King Edward stroked his pointy chin. "Hmmmm. Hmmmm." This reinforced what he'd already heard rumored about the building for the last hour. Lord Earl was not Lord Earl, but detective somebody or other. A pig. Why else would the other pigs be tearing this building apart?

"Hmmmm," King Edward mumbled again, thinking about all the very private things he had confided to Lord Earl over the last few weeks and deciding that he was glad the pig was dead—even if he had suddenly become the prime suspect. "That's right," he said. "But he called it off. That's all I know. I don't know shit."

Ryker was pretty certain that King Edward wasn't the killer, but also knew that there must be something he could say to shed some light on the murder. All King Edward needed was for someone—Ryker, for instance—to jog his memory a bit. Ryker was ready

THE SMACK MAN

to jog. He hit King Edward with his already battered fists, a flurry of hard, deadly punches. King Edward went down like a sack of shit.

The pimp crawled over to a wall and sat himself up. Blood squirted out of his broken nose. "Why you do that for, man? I thought we was partners." He dabbed at his nose with his sleeve.

"King Edward and Count Ryker, Incorporated. Yes, sir. Ass-rubbing buddies. You and me, Eddie." Ryker flexed his right hand. It was swelling after a long afternoon of hard use. "Before I knock your face through that wall, I want you to tell me everything you know about Lord Earl."

King Edward leaned against the wall and told Ryker everything he knew about Lord Earl.

Ryker listened. Every time King Edward's memory went bad, Ryker picked up something like a heavy chrome ashtray or cut-glass cigarette lighter and winged it at the King's head. The King moved his head from side to side to avoid these expensive missiles as they crashed into the wall behind him. His memory got better and better.

Any cops in the hallway hearing the noise would conclude, correctly, that one of the detectives was prompting a stubborn witness.

Ryker sat down on the bottom of an overturned armchair. Nothing King Edward said pointed to any organized crime group. Jealous women? Not likely, Ryker thought. It had to have been somebody whom Williston didn't know or somebody whom he couldn't trust. But somebody who could get past the doorman in the lobby. Ryker stood. "Okay, King. You've been a real help."

THE SMACK MAN

King Edward mumbled something that sounded like "thank you," but wasn't.

Ryker ignored him. His hand hurt worse than the petty insult. He stepped into the hall and rode down the elevator.

No chance that Williston was made for a cop, Ryker thought. He was too good at the game—right down to his lavender silk underwear. And even now he probably wasn't sure. Who else knew?

He slipped out of the lobby unnoticed, and began walking toward the Celite Hotel. York's young ass was definitely hanging in the wind.

She wasn't in the lobby or outside. She must have gotten her first john today, he thought, looking at the fat, greasy man behind the desk. "Where's the whore with the blond hair? The one called Pam?"

The clerk seemed to remember Ryker; he thought he remembered him as a john who, only this morning, had gone with the whore in question. Only he wasn't a cop then. Now he was a cop. No doubt about that. The clerk didn't have to see a badge. "Fucking, I guess. That's what whores do, don't they?"

"Which room?"

The man shrugged. "Don't remember, officer. In fact, I don't remember ever sayin' she was in this hotel. This is a clean—"

Ryker jogged the fat man's memory. He was getting good results with his technique. The clerk bounced off the keyboard behind him; the room keys fell to the floor like tinkling change. The fat man supported himself on the counter. "Jesus Christ, mister. Take it easy."

"Okay. This time I'll hit you easier." Ryker drew his fist back.

The clerk back-pedaled into the keyboard. "Hold on! Room six-twelve," he said, leaning against the counter. His mind was fuzzy; he was seeing double. "Jesus. I can't find the key now." He looked hopelessly at the scattered keys on the floor. He glanced over his shoulder to speak to the cop, but he was gone.

Ryker paused outside of 612 for a moment. Knock or kick? If he kicked it in, he would look like a jealous lover, which he wasn't. He knocked.

A male voice. "Who is it?"

"Ryker."

"Who?"

Mumbled voices behind the door. The door opened. "Come in," Pamela York said. She was wearing a silk blouse and pleated skirt now. She was in her stocking feet. Lying on the bed was a man of about twenty-five, wearing the clothes of a Department of Sanitation worker. Ryker wondered how these guys decided what to wear each morning. He went in.

The man rose slowly, almost insolently. He held out his hand half-heartedly. "Sergeant Ryker? Ted Steele, Anti-Crime. Garbageman," he added with a half smile. "The lady says you're her partner."

Ryker ignored the hand. "Thank you for stopping by, officer. Goodbye."

The man dropped his hand quickly and broke eye contact. He grabbed his hat off the bed and walked to the door. He looked at Pamela York, who had said nothing so far. "Take it easy, Pam."

"You too, Ted."

He slammed the door as he left.

She looked angrily back at Ryker. "What the hell is the meaning of this?"

"Sit down."

"Like hell. You smell like a cop today. A jealous one at that. You probably blew my cover downstairs. Why are—"

"Williston is dead."

She stared at him.

"Shot in the head through the peephole at his apartment."

She backed up and supported herself against the door.

"Sometime between two and three o'clock, I figure."

She put her face in her hands; she began shaking.

Ryker took out a cigar and lit it. "No idea who could have done it? I'll call the PDU later and see what they've developed. Any ideas?" Ryker looked at her as he smoked. Still a female underneath. Crying. But no audible sobs. A lot of men cry too, he thought. Fernandez had been crying. He wanted to tell her it would be all right, but it wouldn't.

Pamela York dropped her hands to her sides. Her face was wet. She fought for control. Her voice quavered. "He was—good. Good to me."

"He was a good man," Ryker agreed. His mind flashed ahead. Another police funeral. He didn't own a dark summer suit. It was a hot September. Where would the funeral be? Probably Queens. Would there be police buses or would everyone have to make it on his own? Police buses, he decided. Thoughts. Distracted and irrelevant. His mind was still trying to take it all in. He stared at the floor.

Suddenly, without his being aware of it, Pamela

York was in his arms. She was sobbing audibly now. "I feel—lonely—scared. What kind of life is this? What —friends killed. Betrayals. Deceptions. Play-acting. Prostitution. Dope—" Her body heaved.

Ryker flipped his ash on the floor. He thought Pamela York was asking pretty stupid questions. Not stupid in themselves, maybe, but stupid because they came so late. He had stopped asking himself questions like that while he was still a rookie. To ask them now after all these years—he felt her grip tighten around his body. He lifted her slightly and put her gently on the bed.

The late-afternoon sun had sunk low, and the room was in semidarkness. On the bed, Pamela York looked suddenly too young, too vulnerable. Silent tears streamed down her cheeks. He knew she was crying not only for Williston, but for herself as well. Tears for a wasted youth—wasted on the streets in pursuit of junkies and pushers.

When he walked back to the bed, she was already unbuttoning her blouse. She did it slowly, mechanically, staring up at the ceiling as though she was not even aware of his presence. Or as though they were old lovers. No coyness. No tease. No passion. It was as though she had made a bet with him and had lost. In a way, that was exactly what had happened. Now she owed him. And she was going to pay.

She sat up and slipped her blouse off. Then unhooked her bra. Her white breasts were high and firm. No bra needed, really. She unzipped her skirt and pulled it down over her legs along with her panties and pantyhose. She kicked them onto the floor. She never once looked at him.

Ryker regarded the firm, milky-white body. Her

flat, muscled stomach was rising and falling. She brought her head forward and rested it on her upraised knees.

Ryker tossed his cigar in the ashtray, then began taking his clothes off, dropping them on the floor next to hers. He went to the foot of the bed and pulled her down and straight on the bed, then spread her well-formed legs. As he laid himself on top of her, she suddenly and unexpectedly grabbed his buttocks and pulled him into her. In spite of her apparent lack of passion, she was very wet. He slid in easily.

Ryker stretched out, took a short drag of her cigarette, and handed it back. The late-afternoon sun had sunk into New Jersey and the room was dark except for the neon lights flashing through the window. The colored signs made patterns across Pamela York's white body. It had rained and the cool, damp air was blowing gently through the dusty venetian blinds, making them move and rustle against the faded curtains. Ryker looked at his watch. Eight o'clock.

York rubbed the sleep from her eyes. "Jesus. The whole fucking force is probably looking for us by now." Her voice had a strange quality to it.

Ryker tried to read something in her voice—in the intimate gesture of sharing a cigarette. He still couldn't completely make her out. She remained a mystery to him. A lot of years on the street, Ryker thought. A lot of make-believe love and a lot of make-believe hate. It confused the senses and the emotions. She probably didn't know herself what she felt. He shrugged to himself in the darkness.

"I don't think so," he said aloud. "They know

damn well I'm up here and you're up here. They've already been in the lobby by now. They just wrote us off for the time being."

"Are we in trouble?" Her voice was serious, then she laughed at the absurdity of the remark.

"What difference does it make?" He yawned. "Who cares? They're through with us and our grand plan anyway." He rolled over. "I'm going back to sleep." He dropped the cigarette into an ashtray on the nightstand.

"Shouldn't we be doing something?"

"I don't know. I can't think with my clothes off."

She smiled into the darkness. Then suddenly, she sat up. "Jesus Christ. I forgot."

"What?" Ryker said, incuriously.

"What time is it?"

"Eight," he said.

"Shit. I have to meet somebody at eight-thirty."

"Where?" Ryker was going to say "who," but that would have been the wrong thing to say after they had just finished making love. He didn't want her to think he was that involved.

"Morningside Park. At 116th Street."

"Why way up there?"

"That's where he hangs out. I think he lives there, too," she said.

"Who?" *He? There it was.* It was his detective's instinct. For almost twenty years on the job he had been asking "who" questions. He told himself he really didn't care who she was going to meet. Or why. It was a lie.

York turned her head and looked at him lying on the sheets. She could see he was ready for sex again. She knew it wouldn't take much to talk her into a quickie, so she swung her legs over the side of the bed. "J.C. Jesus. That's his name. Looks a little like Him." She stood up.

"Puerto Rican?"

"No. Jewish, as a matter of fact."

"I always wondered why, if Jesus' parents were Jewish, they gave Him a Puerto Rican name. Now here's another one."

She laughed. "That's just a street name."

Ryker stretched. "I'm going to stay here. I need some sleep."

"Okay." She fumbled around on the floor and extracted her clothes from his. "But you're welcome to come. It's only business."

No answer.

She threw her clothes on the bed. "I met him this morning for the first time in years. Strange." She turned her pantyhose right-side out. "He walked right up to me in front of the hotel here and started to say something. He didn't recognize me at first and I didn't recognize him. He's grown a beard and it's been about three years." She sat down on the bed and slipped the pantyhose on. The bed creaked.

Ryker put his hands behind his head and closed his eyes.

"I told him what we were doing and everything—"

Ryker shot up. "What!"

She looked over her shoulder. "Oh. I forgot to tell you. He's a cop. Narcotics. Undercover."

Ryker fell back on the bed. "You tell stories ass-backwards." He closed his eyes and began to breathe deeply.

Pamela hooked her bra and began searching for her blouse in the darkness. "He said he heard about the case, of course, and he said he had a lead. He was going to report it to Narcotics, but he'd just as soon give it to us to develop." She slipped on her blouse. "What do you think I should do now? Everything's come apart."

Ryker yawned again. "Well, I'd go to the meet anyway. You never know."

"Right. Can't stand him up."

Ryker grunted.

"He may have something," she continued. "We can pass it on to our replacements. I think our asses are out. What do you think?" She finished buttoning her blouse.

Ryker became more aware of his throbbing penis. He rolled over on his stomach again and buried his head in the pillow. "Who gives a shit?"

Pamela York stood up and shook out her skirt. She already had a few bedbug bites. "You're a real dedicated cop, Ryker."

"Fuck cops," he mumbled into the pillow. He raised his head. "Tell you something—you have more dedication and more balls than me, going into Morningside Park after dark."

She laughed. "I used to sleep there. Besides, I have Mr. Smith and Mr. Wesson with me. So does J.C., of course." She zipped up her skirt. "I'll be fine."

Ryker began breathing heavily, pretending to be asleep.

Pamela York picked up his clothes from the floor and put them on the bed. She placed his shoulder holster with the big .357 Ruger Magnum on the pillow next to him. She also took his service revolver from the chair and put it on the bed. She noticed an unholstered snub-nosed .38 on the chair, too, and was going to ask him about it, but she bent down and kissed him on the shoulder. "I'll see you later," she whispered.

Ryker smiled to himself and was actually asleep before she had gone.

FOURTEEN

Ryker slept badly. He tossed fitfully across the bed; his mind was full of things like death and dope. He dreamed of Christ shooting heroin. Christ saying, "This is good shit, man." His mind raced from one nightmarish scene to the next. He suddenly opened his eyes. The room was very dark; his body was covered with sweat.

Something had clicked in his mind while he was sleeping, but now it was gone. Lost. He held his head. Pain shot through his skull. Something was there—just on the other side of the black curtain.

He sat up in bed and relit a dead cigar from the ashtray. The taste of the cigar matched the foul taste in his mouth. He looked at his watch: 9 P.M. *Jesus,* he thought, *I've got to call Beverly.* He grabbed the phone.

"Gimme an outside line," he said to the desk clerk, who only laughed.

"Use the fucking pay phone like everybody else," he said.

THE SMACK MAN

"Scumbag," Ryker said, and threw the receiver on the floor. It took him only minutes to get dressed.

In the lobby, he saw at once that the fat, greasy desk clerk had been replaced by a tall, cadaverous young man who looked like he was dying of AIDS. Ryker flexed his bruised and cut fists and decided not to jog this man's memory. He didn't want any of the clerk's tainted blood to seep into his own bloodstream.

Ryker walked out into the cold, clammy air, looking for a working pay phone. He spotted a bar called Nico's. Inside, a hundred or so leather queens were dancing and partying, pretending to be macho. Ryker closed the door and walked west on Houston until he came to a pizza parlor. It reminded him he was hungry, so he ordered a slice of mushroom and anchovy pizza, flashed his tin, and asked to use the house phone.

"Hi, babe," he said, munching on his pizza. "Can't make it tonight, after all."

Beverly Kim said all the right things to him, then concluded with a long sigh. "I've missed you."

"Me, too," he said, thinking about Pamela York. "But you know the job. I'll call you tomorrow. I want to hear all about the trip."

He hung up and dialed his ex-wife, Eleanor, planning to tell her he would be glad to go to Chicago, if he could bring a friend. He wanted to rub Pamela York in her face. A strangely erotic thought, he realized. He reversed the charges.

"Hi, babe," he said.

"Oh, Joe, I'm so glad you called," Eleanor said. "It's terrible."

"What?" he asked, recognizing the pain in her voice. "What's wrong?"

THE SMACK MAN

"It's Pablo, Joe, he's . . . he's—"

"Dead?" Ryker asked.

"Worse. He's married," she said.

"Yeah?" Ryker had to control his laughter. He took a big bite of pizza.

"Well, not really married. But he's not divorced yet, and he was ready to marry me before he was legal," she said.

"Mmm," Ryker said, his mouth full of anchovies, mushrooms, and cheese.

"He said it was only a Mexican marriage, Joe, but I feel so . . . so used and lied to," she said. "He never told me."

"Well, you know those macho foreigners. He doesn't wear leather, does he?" Ryker asked, thinking of Nico's.

"Leather?"

"Never mind. Look, Ellie, I got to run now, but I'll call you tomorrow and we'll have a nice long talk. Okay?"

"I've been such a fool, Joe," she said, wanly. "You were right all along."

"I'm always right," he said, wondering if that were *ever* true. He was glad just to maintain the status quo.

He hung up and was just taking another bite of his pizza when a skinny man with shoulder-length hair and a long, scraggily beard lurched into the restaurant. He was drunk or high or both, Ryker decided.

"Attention, attention," the man shouted. "Give me money. I'm askin' nicely cuz I don' wanna haveta rob youse outside. I'm doin' you a favor, so give me money and I'll go away."

"I kick your butt and you'll go away," Ryker said, reaching for his badge. But before he could pull the tin from his pocket, something clicked in his mind. The man's wild eyes and matted beard reminded him of something . . . something York had said. What was it?

J.C. Jesus Christ. Beard. J.C. J.C. Jessie. Street name. He walked right up to me in front of the hotel here and started to say something. Didn't recognize me. He's grown a beard. Narcotics undercover. Meet in Morningside Park. Has a lead. Told him all about it. Williston.

Was it possible? Ryker wondered. Yes. No. He tried to clear his head. What else did she say? What was it? He had to get to Morningside Park.

Benny Schwartz sat on a rock outcrop and picked at his beard. The night had turned clear and fresh after the rain. He scratched a scab on his knee. "So somebody killed this undercover pimp, huh?"

Pamela York wrapped her arms around her knees. She nodded her head sadly. Poor Williston, she thought.

The last of the summer insects were making an uproar against the background of a Puerto Rican salsa group a few hundred yards away. The rock and grass were still wet from the rain. The park was almost deserted.

"So your partner—what's his name, there—Ryker—he didn't want to come here. He's coming later, maybe?" Schwartz asked casually.

"No. He was—asleep."

Benny smiled through his beard. "Ah. I see."

Pamela smiled also. "So what did you want to tell me?"

"Oh, yeah." He cracked his knuckles. "About the guy who's killing the junkies, you mean?"

THE SMACK MAN

"That's the guy."

"You know—I wonder why all the fuss about this guy. Is what he's doing really so bad? I think maybe he's doing a favor for everyone."

"Don't start that crap with me too, Benny. You sound like Ryker. I don't want to hear it. You said you had something."

"Okay. I thought maybe you would see things differently. I thought maybe—well, okay. Never mind."

Pamela York looked at him across the short, flat rock. "Look, if you have something, then you can't hold it back. Why would you want to hold it back?"

"You know. We fight a losing battle in this business. Every year the junk destroys more and more people. Worse yet are the bastards who make fortunes from this stuff, this junk. Did you know that my sister—?"

"I heard about it. I'm sorry," York said.

"She died a junkie and a whore."

"I know."

"And now my young brother. Last time I saw him, he looked like a zombie. A robot. Lifeless. He steals from my poor mother to buy the junk. And me, a law enforcement officer, yet." He laughed bitterly.

"I didn't know about your brother."

Benny went on as though he hadn't heard her. "And they get rich. The pushers. They rake in the money. And the junkies steal and whore for money. The men would crush your skull for a fix, and the girls, they fuck. Good girls before the junk."

"We all know the problem, Benny. But come on— you don't kill people just because they're junkies or pushers."

"Yes, you do," he said.

THE SMACK MAN

York took a breath; a chill ran up her spine.

Benny smiled. "You would have figured it out yourself. Tomorrow. It would hit you—pow—like that. Like it hit you now. I thought maybe you knew right away. When I met you on the street. Williston. He knew. I could tell when I talked to him on the phone this afternoon. I knew he knew by his voice. I didn't want to have to—but okay. So now it has to be done. Again." He sounded sad. Tired.

York heard the double click of a revolver. She looked at the gun. Hard to make out in this light, she thought. Big and long. Not his .38 Special. A clean gun, probably. She looked down at her pocketbook sitting on the rock a few feet from her. Not a chance.

Benny sighed. "Such a pretty girl, too." His voice became hard. "And this Ryker. He will know also. So he will have to die, too." He sighed again. "So much death. A very clever trap you had, but you didn't think you would catch Benny Schwartz in the net, did you? As it turned out, however, you did, and when you did, you didn't even think you had caught anything. You were ready to throw me back. You thought you had the wrong fish."

"But you knew about the plan, Benny." Her voice was soft—controlled. "You must have been told." She needed time. Ryker would know. He would figure it out if he weren't still sleeping. She cursed herself for her stupidity. She cursed herself for telling Schwartz about Williston's undercover role. Did she tell Ryker where the meet would take place? She couldn't remember.

"Oh. You know how it is. Deep undercover. You don't get back to the squad room much. You don't read the memos. You don't pay attention to the talk.

THE SMACK MAN

You start acting alone, more and more. Bad mistake. I shoulda known. I shoulda kept my eyes and ears open for this kind of thing."

"Benny—listen," she said. "Let's talk it over some more. Maybe I do see your point." Time. Faced with death, the natural reaction is to buy time. A few seconds. Try to buy time, borrow time, steal time. Without cringing—without crawling. Calm, reasonable voice. "We've known each other a lot of years, Benny. If you really believe in what you're doing, maybe I'll believe too."

Benny scratched his head. "Too late, Pam." He pulled a pair of handcuffs out of his waistband. He threw them to her. "Put them on. Behind your back. Quick."

She hesitated. Stalled. Began to argue. Buy time. Maybe a passing stroller would show up. Maybe a police patrol. Something. Anything.

Benny shook his head. "Put them on, please."

She clipped one cuff around her wrist and put her hands behind her back. She clipped the other around her free wrist. Shackled. No chance at all now. Time. All she needed was time.

"Please, Benny," she pleaded. "Talk to me. Tell me why you're doing this."

Benny bit his thumbnail. "I suppose I owe you some explanation," he said. "I feel real safe about telling you everything—about how I hijacked the money for the heroin down in Chinatown, about how I killed those four Chinks and everybody thought it was a tong war." He bit down hard and the blood seeped from his torn thumb, and he was silent.

"Tell me, Benny," she pleaded.

THE SMACK MAN

"Not much to tell," he said. "Once I had the junk, I cut it with strychnine, and began peddling it to hookers. Greedy bitches couldn't get enough." He laughed bitterly.

"Benny—"

"Talk's over," he said.

He stood up slowly and stretched. Then he walked casually across the flat rock and made a quick, catlike movement. The leather blackjack hit her a glancing blow behind her head. It would leave no telltale marks or bruises.

Benny guided York down as she slumped to her knees. He knelt, put her carefully on her side and looked at her face.

She was stunned, but still conscious. In her numbed brain she knew what type of death to expect. She began to mumble. So little time.

Benny reached under her dress and pulled her panties and pantyhose down to her ankles. From under his shirt, he extracted a glass hypodermic needle. He wiped his prints from it, held the needle with a handkerchief and carefully touched the hypodermic to her fingertips.

She began moving. Rolling. Struggling. She started sobbing softly. Very little time left.

Benny held her down with his knees. He moved a lighter under the hypodermic for a few seconds and heated the liquid right in the syringe. He ran his dirty fingers over her thigh. He found her surgically-induced railroad tracks in the half-light.

Her mind was clearing. "Benny. Please. Not like this. Please!" A few more seconds, please.

He bent over and placed a soft, tender kiss on her

cheek, and at the same time jabbed the needle into her thigh. He pushed the plunger and let go of the needle. "Peace." He unlocked the cuffs, then stood and stepped back.

Pamela York lay still for a moment. Her chest heaved. She rolled onto her back and the needle fell out of her thigh onto the rock. She drew her legs up as though she wanted to pull up her panties. Suddenly, her body jerked, like a fish out of water. It jerked and snapped. A long strangling, suffocating sound gurgled from her throat. Her arms and legs flailed wildly; her back arched in a bow.

Benny could hear the sound of cracking bones.

Pamela York lay still. Her time had run out.

"Peace," he said quietly.

She was bent and contorted like a broken doll. Her shoes and underwear had flown off and lay obscenely in the bushes. Benny's eyes misted. He looked around to make sure everything was in order, stuffed Pamela York's pocketbook under his shirt, then began walking toward busy Amsterdam Avenue, a few hundred yards away. With a lot of luck the police would just look at her whore clothes, makeup, and railroad tracks, do an autopsy and dump her in Potter's Field. With a little less luck, she would somehow be identified. The police brass would then have to decide if she, one, was a junkie all along and got hold of some of the bad junk; two, committed suicide; or three, was the victim of foul play. In any case, Benny knew that he was pretty much in the clear. Only this guy Ryker might know something. Only Ryker and Williston, as far as Benny could determine, knew about this meeting. He had to find Ryker before Ryker came looking for him.

Benny reached Amsterdam Avenue and mixed into

the passing street crowd. He became another bearded young man among all the other bearded young men on the sidewalk.

Ryker found her on the rock in Morningside Park at 10 P.M., thirty minutes after she had died. He sat next to her body for a long time and smoked a cigar. He sat staring at her twisted body. Her skirt was raised and her legs were spread in an obscene position. He fought the impulse to lower her skirt. It was a stupid impulse, he told himself. Almost twenty years on the force and he still had the impulse to lower skirts on female corpses. He wondered if he was getting too soft for the job. He wished he could be like Fernandez and let the tears come. But he couldn't.

He reflected on the facts of the case as he had them. J.C., or whatever he called himself, was smart. Ryker doubted if York's or Williston's murder could be pinned on him, let alone all the murders of the junkies. The only solution seemed to be to find J.C., and kill him. It was logical and sensible, he thought.

Ryker got up, took a last look at Pamela York and walked through the silent park to 116th Street. He found a phone booth and anonymously reported the location of the body.

Next, he called Narcotics and after fifteen minutes of transferred calls and making proper identification, he spoke with a Captain Gambini. He identified himself for the tenth time.

"Okay, Sergeant," Gambini said. "It's been checked out already. Calm down. We can't be too careful, you know. Lots of weirdos call here. Your people are on the other line."

THE SMACK MAN

"My people? You mean the Rykers? Tell them to go fuck themselves."

"No. I mean your PDU. A Lieutenant Fischetti. He'd like to know where you are, by the way."

"In a booth," Ryker said. "Listen, time is critical. You have an undercover narc. Young. Bearded—"

"Got lots of them," Gambini said.

"Listen, Goddamnit!" Ryker tried to bring his frustration under control. "Works Manhattan. Times Square—Upper West Side—Harlem, maybe. Maybe lives by Morningside Park. Street name—Jesus Christ, J.C., Jessie, Digger, and Dr Pepper."

There was a long pause. "I don't know all the street names, really," Capt. Gambini said.

"Looks like Christ. Know what Christ looks like, for Christ's sake?" Ryker said.

"Never met Him in person. Let me think," Gambini said.

Ryker waited.

Gambini breathed into the phone. Silence. "A couple of guys, but—"

"He's Jewish. That's another thing. He's Jewish."

"Jewish?"

"Jewish, for Christ's sake, Jewish. How many fucking young bearded undercover Manhattan narcs do you have who are Jewish and look like Jesus Christ and maybe live in Morningside Heights?"

A long pause. "One. Just one I can think of."

"Name."

"Schwartz. Benny Schwartz."

The name meant nothing to Ryker. "I have to find him. Now. Life or death and all that shit," He said.

"Why?" Captain Gambini asked.

THE SMACK MAN

Ryker passed his hand over his face. The cramped, humid booth was suffocating, but the street noise outside made him keep the door closed. "His life's in imminent danger. Great danger."

"From who?"

Ryker wanted to say, "From me, you dumb motherfucker. From me." He thought quickly. "A pusher. A pusher made him. Where could I find him now?"

The captain hesitated. "He keeps a front apartment on West 114th. Near Columbia. He might be there."

"Address?"

The captain hesitated again.

"Come on, for God's sake, Captain. I'm a few blocks from there. I can reach him before you if he's there."

Gambini was in a quandary. Something didn't sound right about this. But maybe a cop's life *was* in danger. Schwartz had no phone in his place. A front for a degenerate junkie would have no phone. He wavered. Then he scribbled a message on a note pad and handed it to a passing sergeant. He covered the mouthpiece. "Get this on the air. 10-13. No sirens. That's 532 West 114th. Quick."

Ryker felt the captain slipping away. "If Schwartz gets wasted, it's your ass, Gambini."

"Okay, 532 West 114th. Apartment C-3. If you're not on the level, you son of a—"

Ryker hung up. He threw open the door of the phone booth and began running down Amsterdam Avenue. Less than two blocks to 114th. He knew there would be a 10-13 out in a matter of seconds. If there were no cars in the area, he would get there first. If Benny Schwartz wasn't at his place, then he'd have crapped out. The police would find Schwartz before he did.

One hundred fifteenth Street. Columbia was on his right as he ran. People scurried out of his way and stared after him as he flew by. He had four minutes at best.

But was Benny Schwartz his man? Did he have enough time to find out before the cops arrived? He'd had to say too much to Gambini. Now the entire department was on to him. It wouldn't take long for Narcotics to start comparing notes with his PDU. Pamela York's body in Morningside Park. Ryker's strange phone call to Narcotics. Bearded man. Benny Schwartz. Even an idiot like Fischetti could figure out the connection, and even Fischetti could figure out what was going to happen next.

If Ryker didn't find Schwartz at home, then he swore he would find a way—any way—to kill him.

One hundred fourteenth Street. The end of Columbia University. Ryker grabbed at the street pole on the run and swung west. He began running down 114th Street. 512. 522. 532. Old tenements. Semi-deserted. Five-story walk-up. No police cars in sight.

Ryker leaped up the steps and pushed open the outer door. The inner door was locked. Diamond-paned glass. He crashed through the door like it was made of paper and ran up the stairs. He felt a warm stickiness under his clothes; his throbbing heart pumped the blood to the surface and out through the ugly glass cuts. Third floor. C-3. He hit the door with tensed muscles, adrenalin flowing and heart pounding.

He shoulder-rolled across the floor of the half-darkened room and drew his .357 Magnum from his shoulder holster. A foot kicked his arm; the gun flew across the floor. Then the toe of a shoe caught him in the eye. Ryker lay on his stomach and looked up.

Benny Schwartz was holding a big ugly-looking piece on him. "Ryker, I presume? You made a lot of noise charging up here, schmuck. Somehow I knew it was a caller for me. I didn't expect you so soon, though."

Ryker could feel his eye closing. A blinding, searing pain ran through his skull; blood ran down his cheek. His breath came in short spurts. "Motherfucker."

"You alone?"

"Fuck you."

The sound of cars screeching to a halt in the street came through the open window.

Ryker looked up at Schwartz. "Pull the trigger, you motherfucking bastard. Then they'll really have something to hang your ass with."

Running footsteps on the pavement below.

"Not really, Sergeant. I shot an intruder. Excessive force, maybe. Overreaction. I'll take that rap. Didn't know it was a cop. Busting through my door like that."

Loud footsteps in the foyer below.

"Then shoot, you fuck," Ryker growled. "It's over for you one way or the other. Everyone's on to you, prick."

"I doubt that."

Running footsteps on the stairs.

"Peace." Benny Schwartz cocked the big pistol.

Footsteps running down the hall.

"A lot of time went by since your neighbors heard

THE SMACK MAN

your door come crashing down," Ryker said. "You're going to have trouble explaining why you took so long to shoot, asshole."

Schwartz nodded and uncocked the pistol. "I think I'll take my chances in court."

Two patrolmen appeared at the door, guns drawn.

Schwartz was holding his badge up high in one hand, his pistol in the other raised hand. "Police officer! Narcotics undercover! Don't shoot!"

The two policemen were crouched at the door, nervously waving their guns between Ryker's prostrate form and Schwartz.

"Drop it! Drop it!" one cop yelled. More uniformed police appeared in the hall. Neighbors' voices could be heard now.

Schwartz dropped the gun. "A dumb mistake has been made, boys. I'm on the job. So is this gentleman on the floor, I think." He smiled at Ryker.

"Where's the cop in trouble?" a late-arriving patrolman shouted. "Where's the 10-13?"

"Beats me," Benny said. "First I heard of it."

EPILOGUE

It has been said that a grand jury will return an indictment against a ham sandwich, and in fact, one inattentive group of citizens once actually voted to indict one "A. Ham Sandwich," much to the delight of prosecutors and defense attorneys alike.

Benny Schwartz was much luckier. The grand jury found no evidence of any heroin, poisoned or otherwise, in his apartment or on his person. A few witnesses, all prostitutes, claimed to have seen Benny selling heroin, but that, after all, was part of his undercover work, and the whores made terrible witnesses.

Worse, no one saw Benny at My Place the day Williston died—or claimed not to have seen him. So that was the ballgame. No indictment. Officer Benny Schwartz was a free man.

Ryker wasn't so lucky.

Whenever a police officer dies, somebody gets charged with something. In this case two cops had died and Ryker looked like a good candidate for a departmental. The charges were vague, but a police trial didn't require the same evidence as a criminal trial. Ryker was found guilty and given a one-month suspension.

Wondering how he could while away the time until he returned to duty, Ryker called his ex-wife Eleanor, and arranged to fly to Chicago to meet her. He canceled his plans at the last moment, however, when Beverly Kim invited him on a sun-drenched vacation for two.

Benny Schwartz resigned from the force soon after the grand jury action. He was found dead—shot to death—in a rented house outside of Ft. Lauderdale a few days before Ryker's suspension ended.

When Ryker returned to his PDU, a few detectives remarked kiddingly about the nice tan he had gotten during his suspension.